THE SURREY STALKER

A DCI ROB MILLER MYSTERY

B.L. PEARCE

1

The stalker watched as the object of his attention exited the National Archives building in Kew, West London, a little after six o'clock in the evening, her handbag slung casually over her shoulder.

Right on schedule.

She glanced up at the April sky and frowned at the ominous clouds that threatened to erupt at any given moment. It was still light, but only just. The sun had already set and what little light was left was hastily following its descent into darkness.

She hesitated. The stalker knew what she was thinking.

Should I take the river path to the right which is quicker but more isolated, or should I stick to the main roads, which are safer but will add fifteen minutes to my walk home?

She turned right, opting for speed over security.

The stalker smiled to himself.

Perfect.

He followed her around the brutalist building with its gun-metal grey chunks of concrete and complex spaces casting long, chaotic shadows across the surrounding lawns. She walked fast, her jacket pulled tight around her slender frame. He could hear her heels crunching on the gravel path as she made her way towards the river.

He knew her route by heart. She'd follow the towpath along the Thames for just under a mile after which she'd climb the steps to Kew Bridge, cross it, and turn left into Brentford. Her apartment was off Brentford High Street, a new tower block with a cold, characterless exterior and shaded glass windows. It had probably been advertised as having a river view, but her apartment didn't. It faced the wrong way.

As she turned onto the river path, the heavens opened, and the rain began bucketing down. The stalker hung back as she fiddled in her handbag for an umbrella.

"Come on..." he muttered, watching her launch it against the deluge.

Then she was off again.

The towpath was pretty secluded along this stretch, which was why he'd chosen it. On the right-hand side was the river, swollen and about to burst its banks, while on the left, an impenetrable tangle of trees and foliage backed onto allotments. There was nobody around thanks to the weather and the high tide. Except her, of course.

It was the perfect killing ground.

The stalker narrowed the distance between them, careful to keep to the left where the trees overhung the path. The leaves were only beginning to grow back after a long, frosty winter and the gnarled branches cast twisted patterns onto the gravel. Here, in the shadow of the foliage, she wouldn't see him approaching. He wore soft-soled trainers to mask his footsteps, and where he could, trod on tufts of grass and fallen leaves.

The moment of truth was approaching. She was almost there, at the point where the allotments ended, and the field began, where the trees were thicker and the undergrowth deeper. The point of no return, he called it. The point where he had to act, or the opportunity would be lost.

Sure, there would always be another night, but this one was perfect. It was as if the universe was working with him. The weather, the timing and her decision to take the river path, all colluded to create the perfect opportunity. He wasn't going to waste it.

His heart rate quickened along with his pace. Keeping his back to the undergrowth he almost ran the last few metres but forced himself to keep steady in case she heard him. He needn't have bothered. She was oblivious to any sound other than her heeled boots on the gravel and the rain pummelling down on her umbrella.

This was it, the moment he had been waiting for. The moment where he would make her pay. The stalker took one last look around him, checking the path was deserted. It was.

Time to strike.

He lunged at his target, putting one hand over her mouth and the other around her neck. He felt hot breath against his palm as she tried to scream. She dropped her umbrella and struggled against him, but he was so much stronger than her, it hardly seemed a fair fight. Within seconds, he'd pulled her into the undergrowth. It was wild and bushy and swallowed them up almost immediately.

A runner jogged by, taking the stalker by surprise. He fell to his knees, taking the buckling woman with him. A wet branch smacked them in the face before they landed on the sodden ground. She tried to shout out, but he clamped down harder over her mouth and the jogger didn't hear her muffled moan. He ran past with only a cursory glimpse at the abandoned umbrella, oblivious to the woman being attacked only yards away.

That was close.

She wouldn't stop wriggling, so he tightened his hold around her neck until he felt her strength ebb away. A few more seconds and she would be unconscious.

There.

He laid her gently on the mulch-covered ground and studied her face, breathing hard. Her eyes were shut, and her chest rose and fell in an even rhythm like she was asleep. She looked so tranquil with her wet hair spread out against the dark leaves and her pale skin dripping with rain. She would look that way again once he was done with her.

But first, he would make her pay.

JULIE WOKE with a gasp as cold air filled her lungs. She looked wildly around her, the memory of the attack flooding back. Where was she? All she could see was wet foliage.

"Welcome back," said a voice that seemed to hover somewhere above her.

She blinked against the rain. It was dark, and she couldn't see a face, just two eyes staring down at her. For a moment, she thought she'd been abducted by some supernatural being, then she realised her assailant was wearing a balaclava. Terror rose up and threatened to choke her. She opened her mouth to scream, but he anticipated it and stuck tape over it rendering her cries useless. Julie tried to move but her hands were tied together above her head. They wouldn't budge. He must have secured her to a branch or a tree stump or something. She lashed out with her legs, noticing with alarm that he'd removed her boots. Her legs kicked air. He laughed and sat down on top of her.

"There's no escape, you may as well relax and enjoy it."

He began to undo his jeans.

Oh, God. He's going to rape me.

Julie felt sick. Nausea rose into her throat and she began heaving against the gag. She lifted her head to stem the rising tide.

"Settle down," he whispered, forcing her head back down against the ground. Then, he pushed her dress up and ripped off her underwear. The rain felt wet and cold on her bare legs.

Please, she wanted to beg. *Please, don't do this.*

But she couldn't speak.

She heard the sound of a wrapper and knew he was putting on a condom. His hands slid between her thighs, pushing them apart. She tried to resist, but he was too strong. He kneed her in the groin and the pain made her wince. She fought savagely, but he had her pinned down. She could hear him panting above her, his acrid breath on her face.

"Keep still," he growled, "or I'll hurt you even more."

She ignored him and bucked like a bronco, until one of her legs got free. Then she connected with bare flesh.

"Shit. You bitch!" A hard fist smacked into her face. She felt blood spurt from her nose. Her vision clouded, and it was only the cold rain that kept her from blacking out.

In a haze, she watched him pull down his jeans, put on the condom and straddle her. She writhed uselessly as she felt him enter her, desperately trying to shout out against the gag.

It hurt.

She squeezed her eyes shut against the pain, trying to block it out. With her nose filled with blood and the gag over her mouth, it was hard to breathe. She began to panic, thinking she might suffocate.

She thought of Justin. Darling Justin, waiting for her to come home. He said he'd have supper ready, a bottle of champagne, and their own private celebration.

Now it would never happen. She'd never know what it was like being Justin's wife. The mother of his children.

Tears ran down her face.

Dinner would go cold. Justin would wonder where she was. Then worry would set in. He'd call her mobile, then her work.

She left hours ago, Ziv, the doorman would tell him.

The police would be called.

Her attacker's motions grew more and more frantic and she knew he was nearing the end.

He began to make a low, rasping sound, and then she felt his hands close around her neck. He needn't have bothered, she was suffocating anyway, the lack of oxygen making her dizzy. But they clamped down until she couldn't breathe at all anymore.

"Bridget," she heard him gasp as he squeezed the last dregs of life out of her, and then she succumbed to the darkness.

2

R ob Miller rolled off Yvette, a smile on his face. "You're amazing." He bent his head to kiss her full on the lips.

She smiled a slow, satisfied smile and kissed him back. "You aren't so bad yourself."

He stroked her breast, his hand moving over the blood-red lace bra which she'd left on during their lovemaking. "And I definitely appreciate the perks of your job."

The matching panties were discarded somewhere at the foot of the bed.

Yvette purred like a cat then pushed herself up onto the pillows. "You should see what I've got 'idden away for the wedding night." Her French accent made it sound sexier.

Rob groaned. "You're torturing me, you know that?"

There was a packet of cigarettes lying on the bedside table and Yvette leaned over, took one out with her long, elegant fingers and lit it. "That's the idea."

She exhaled, letting a slow spiral of smoke escape from her mouth. Rob watched it drift up to the ceiling, wishing he could have a drag. He'd given up four months ago as a New Year resolution, just to prove to himself that he could, and he was determined not to give in so soon. He had a bet going with Luke, a DS at the station, to see who could last the longest. So far neither of them had wavered. Any motivation was good motivation in his book.

Yvette didn't see the point in quitting smoking. "Do you want me to get fat and ugly?" she'd asked when he'd suggested they give up together. "Because that is what will 'appen if I stop." Yvette fat and ugly? That would be the day. She was far too weight-conscious to allow that to happen, but he hadn't pushed her on it.

A former lingerie model, she now worked at Harrods as a sales assistant, but she still took excellent care of her body. He often came home to find her doing yoga on the lounge floor, twisting herself into a position a contortionist would be proud of. To be honest, he couldn't believe his luck. Yvette was the kind of woman men salivated over in glossy magazines. What she saw in him, he had no idea, all he knew was, he didn't want it to stop.

"Why don't we go to that little French bistro in Richmond tonight?" She admired the engagement ring on her finger. "We can celebrate, just the two of us." Her nails were long and the colour of Cabernet Sauvignon. The cigarette burned down between them. She took another drag.

"Sounds good," said Rob, just as his phone rang. He glanced at the caller ID and held up a finger. "Hold that thought."

Yvette's smile disappeared, and she gazed out of the window. It was dark outside, the sun having set hours ago, yet the curtains were still open. They hadn't got around to closing them before lust had overwhelmed them.

"DI Rob Miller," he said.

It was his boss, DCI Sam Lawrence. "Rob, a body has been found on the towpath in Kew. A female, looks like she's been strangled and possibly sexually assaulted. It's yours if you want it."

Rob didn't need to think about it. He'd been waiting for an

opportunity like this for a while. It was high-time he was made SIO on a murder case. "I'm on my way. What's the address?"

DCI Lawrence gave it to him. "Forensics are already on their way, as is DS Mallory. He'll be your second on this."

"Thanks, guv." Rob put down the phone already dreading Yvette's response. She didn't take kindly to him leaving at all hours of the day and night to go to a crime scene. "I'm sorry." He reached over to squeeze her thigh. "This is a big one."

"No, you're not." She stood up taking most of the sheet with her. "I know you, Robert. You enjoy this sort of thing." She only called him Robert when she was upset with him.

He didn't deny it. "It's my job, Yvette. You know that. It's what I do."

Her lips formed a perfect pout. "But you worked all day. It's seven-thirty. Can't someone else do it? Don't you people work in shifts?"

He kept his voice steady. "I'm a new DI. My boss is giving me a chance to prove myself, he's making me senior investigator on this one. I have to go." Why was that so hard to understand?

His job was one of the few things they argued about, if you could call it arguing. Yvette pouted and complained. He apologised, and she ignored him. So, he went out to work anyway, and when he got back they fell into bed and made up. Thankfully, she never stayed angry for very long.

She shrugged. "I still don't see why one of the other DI's can't go? You are always the first person he phones. It's like you can't wait to get out of here."

He stood up and walked around the bed. "You know that's not true." He reached for her, but she turned away. "I'm going to take a shower."

He sighed and let her go. His phone rang again.

It had begun.

.   .   .

"AT LEAST IT'S STOPPED RAINING," Rob said to Will Mallory as they marched along the Thames towpath towards the crime scene. They both angled their torches on the gravel path ahead, filled with shadows and pockmarks, careful not to trip over any twigs or branches that had fallen during the rainstorm. Mallory was a detective sergeant in his early twenties with prematurely balding hair and a keen, inquisitive face. He'd transferred from Wandsworth last year, but Rob had worked with him before. He was thorough, he followed up on things, and even showed a bit of initiative when it was called for. Rob liked that about him.

"It's down here," puffed Mallory who'd made the trip several times this evening already. "Watch your step, it's muddy. What she was doing walking alone along this stretch after dark is beyond me."

Rob shone his beam to the right where the river was half a metre from the towpath and flowing rapidly downstream like a vast oil-slick. The tide was going out.

"When was she found?" he asked.

"About an hour ago by a dog walker," explained Mallory. "The man lives in the complex behind the allotments and takes his pooch for a walk along this path every evening around six-thirty. He's coming in tomorrow to give an official statement."

At six-thirty he'd been in bed with Yvette, while some poor girl was lying out here having just been murdered. He shivered. "It must have been pouring down then."

"It was, judging by the state of her."

The body was protected by a yellow forensic tent. It glowed eerily against the dripping green backdrop thanks to the emergency lighting that had been set up inside. A police photographer was taking pictures of the scene. Rob could hear the continuous clicking of the lens as he changed into his protective coveralls. Mallory, who'd already been inside once, didn't get changed, but he did pull on a pair of gloves. Rob lifted the flap and was immediately blinded by the glare from the fluorescent bulbs. He blinked several times, then studied the woman lying on the wet ground with her hands tied above her head. She was young, about Mallory's age and very pretty by the looks of it. There was a strip of duct-tape over her mouth and congealed blood clogging her nose. Her dress was twisted around her waist and her underwear was missing. She was naked from the waist down.

Not good.

"Sexual assault?" he asked the pathologist inspecting the body.

"Almost certainly," he acknowledged with a solemn dip of his head. "She was also strangled. See the bruising around her neck?"

"That's how she died?"

"Well, it's the most likely scenario, but with clots in her nose and that gag on, she probably couldn't breathe, anyway."

Rob moved around the body, careful not to touch her, in order to get a better look at her neck. The discolouration was substantial.

"Big hands?"

"Bigger than mine at any rate," said the pathologist, encircling her neck with his own hands to demonstrate. His fingers didn't reach the myriad of bruised and broken veins on the sides. Rob studied the pathologist. He was an average-sized man, maybe five foot ten or eleven, with average-sized hands.

"So, we're looking for a big guy, then?"

The pathologist shrugged. "Theoretically, but then some big guys have small hands and vice versa. You can never tell for sure."

"He punched her in the face?" Rob bent down to inspect her nose."

"Yes, a real bully, this one. Probably to subdue her," remarked the pathologist. "Judging by the bruising on her wrists, she put up one hell of a fight. She's also got cuts and scrapes on the back of her legs where she lashed out."

"Hopefully, we can get some DNA off her," Rob said.

"There's nothing under the fingernails," the pathologist pointed out. "Sorry to disappoint you. He probably secured her hands before she had a chance to retaliate. Also, this rain isn't going to make it easy for us. Any fibres on her skin or clothing may have been washed off."

"What about internally?" Rob glanced at her naked skin. It was demeaning being exposed like that, for everyone to see. His voice tightened. "And can't we cover her up now?"

"I can only tell you that after the post-mortem." The pathologist glanced up at him. "I'm just finishing up, then we'll get her decent again."

Rob nodded and left the tent. He didn't want to look at her anymore, not in that state. The fresh air helped refocus him.

"Do we know who she was?" he asked Mallory, who was waiting a few metres away.

Mallory handed him her driving license. "This was in her wallet. Her handbag was found beside her body."

He glanced at the driving license. "Julie Andrews."

"Like the actress," said Mallory.

"She lives in Brentford," noted Rob.

"We found this too." He passed Rob a laminated access card.

"The National Archives," he read. "That's a short distance back along the path. She must have been walking home from work when she was attacked."

"Silly girl to come this way," remarked Mallory. "It's pitch dark by six p.m. and there's no lighting or CCTV down here."

"Did she have any cash in her wallet?"

"Yeah, twenty pounds and some change. He wasn't after her money."

So, this wasn't a robbery. It was a premeditated attack by a predator on an unsuspecting woman. Opportunistic, or had he been watching her, waiting for his chance to attack?

"He could have been a work colleague," Rob said, thinking out loud. "Someone who knew her and had it in for her. Perhaps a jilted lover?"

"I'll go and talk to her work colleagues tomorrow. See if they know anything."

"That hers?" Rob nodded to a closed, black umbrella in a plastic evidence bag.

"Yup, we think so. It was found open on the path. She could have dropped it when she was attacked. We'll have it tested once we get it to the lab. You never know, she may have whacked him with it."

"Here's hoping," said Rob. He thought for a moment, picturing the series of events. "She was walking home along the river path from Kew to Brentford when this guy attacks her. The towpath was probably deserted on account of the weather, and it would have been high tide which puts off the cyclists. He pulls her into the bushes and subdues her somehow, maybe by punching her in the face, before gagging her and tying her up. Then he rapes and strangles her."

"Fucking bastard," muttered Mallory, shaking his head.

"I wonder what came first," Rob said thoughtfully. "The rape or the strangulation?"

"You mean he could have raped her after he'd killed her?"

Rob nodded. "It's been known to happen."

"Christ."

Mallory might be a good copper, but he was still relatively inexperienced. This was a big case for him too. Both their careers depended on finding the bastard who did this.

3

Rob took family liaison officer, Becca Townsend, with him to notify the next of kin. She was a robust, matronly woman with sympathetic eyes and a compassionate nature. The type of woman you wanted beside you in a crisis. He hadn't worked with her before, but she came highly recommended, particularly considering the violent nature of this attack. Apparently, she'd trained as a rape counsellor before she'd joined the force.

"Mr. Justin King?" he asked when a man in his late twenties, possibly early thirties opened the door.

The man nodded. He wore jeans and a Nike tracksuit top with the tick on it, but still managed to look dishevelled. Maybe it was his hair that stuck up all over the place, or his bare feet, or the confused expression on his face.

"I'm DI Rob Miller and this is DS Becca Townsend with the Richmond Police." Rob showed him his warrant card. Becca did the same. "May we come in?"

He opened the door wordlessly, a haunted expression on his face.

"Thank you," said Becca, offering a small smile. They followed him into a cosy lounge with the television on showing reruns of "Friends". The artificial laughter filled the air.

"Do you mind if we turn that off?" said Becca.

Justin nodded and reached for the control. "I wasn't watching it anyway. Not really. I'm too worried about Julie." He clicked off the TV and they all sat down. Justin gazed from one to the other. "I take it you've got some news?"

Rob nodded. This bit never got easier. He reminded himself that in some cases, the boyfriend or husband was the perpetrator, and not only did they have to be compassionate, but also alert for clues or additional information that might help them solve the case.

"We found a young woman's body this evening by the river towpath in Kew. The evidence suggests that it was Julie."

The young man stared at him uncomprehendingly. Rob was beginning to wonder if he'd heard him. "You reported her missing earlier this evening?"

"Yes, yes..." Justin's eyes filled with tears. "I knew something bad had happened to her. I could sense it. She's never late, not without calling." He dropped his head into his hands while Rob and Becca waited for the news to sink in. It always took a few moments, then the grief or the anger would come to the fore.

"Are you sure it's her?" he asked, eventually. Denial. He couldn't quite grasp that she was dead. Not yet, but that usually ended when they identified the body.

"We're sure," said Becca softly. "She had her purse with her."

Justin let out a slow, shaky breath. It was sinking in.

"How did she die?" he croaked.

"She was strangled," said Rob gently. He hesitated and cast a glance at Becca who gave him a small nod. "There was also evidence of sexual assault."

Justin's head snapped up. "You mean she was raped?"

Rob nodded. "It looks that way. I'm sorry."

"Oh, Christ." He hung his head as the tears rolled down his cheeks. "Poor Julie."

Becca went to sit next to him. "Is there anyone we can call to be with you right now?"

He shook his head. "No, there's no one. I'll have to tell her parents." He gulped. "God knows how I'm going to do that. Her mother will be devastated. They both will."

"We can do that for you, if you like?" said Becca kindly.

He shook his head. "I think it'll be better coming from me."

She nodded. "Okay, but we're here for you if you need to talk."

He nodded. "Can I see her?" he asked.

"Yes, of course. We'd like you to give a formal identification, but it can wait until tomorrow."

"No, I want to see her now. I want to be sure it's... it's her."

"I understand," said Becca. "If you're certain you want to do it now, we can arrange that."

He nodded and stood up. "I'll get my coat."

He walked into the hall and pulled on a navy-blue jacket and picked up the house keys from the side table.

"You'd better put some shoes on." Becca nodded to his bare feet.

"Oh, yeah. Sorry, I'm not thinking straight."

He went upstairs, and they waited. Rob didn't speak. Neither did Becca. This was the very worst part of the job.

Justin came back down wearing trainers but no socks.

"You okay?" said Becca. "Perhaps it would be better to do this in the morning?"

"I want to do it now." Justin jingled the keys in his pocket. "I have to know it's her."

"Okay, let's go."

Rob led the way to the police car outside. They'd left the blue lights on, but no sound came from the sirens. He could see the neigh-bours watching from their bedroom windows. Pale, questioning faces staring down into the street below. It was close to midnight.

They were just about to put Justin into the police car when he turned to Rob and said, "Does this have anything to do with the stalker?"

"What stalker?" asked Rob as soon as they'd got into the car. Becca was driving, so he twisted in his seat to look at Justin who was in the back.

"There was this creepy guy who used to follow her around," Justin explained. "About three weeks ago. He would follow her to work, appear in random places, always watching her. It freaked her out."

"I'm sure it did," said Becca, keeping her eyes on the road. "Did she report him?"

"Yes," said Justin. "I told her to. Stalking is a criminal offence these days."

"It certainly is," Becca confirmed.

"Did she know him?" Rob asked.

"She said she'd never seen him before." Justin looked down at his hands. "One day he just appeared, then she spotted him several times over the next few weeks, but after she reported it, he backed off. We thought he'd given up."

"It may not be connected," said Rob carefully, although he didn't believe it for a second. It was too much of a coincidence. "But we'll definitely look into it."

Justin nodded. The look on his face said, *fat lot of good it'll do her now.*

Becca took Justin to the mortuary to identify the body of Julie Andrews, while Rob went back to the station. Despite it being after one am, the whole team was there including DCI Sam Lawrence.

"Now you're back we can have a briefing," he barked. "Incident room two, please guys."

They all filed in. The few chairs in the room were filled quickly, while everyone else stood in eager anticipation. Rob's mobile phone beeped. He glanced at the screen. It was Yvette. He ignored the message and went to stand beside DCI Lawrence at the front of the room. Someone, probably Mallory, had pinned two photographs of Julie Andrews up on the whiteboard. One was a normal, happy shot, the 'before-shot', while the other, the 'after-shot', had been taken at the crime scene. Underneath was a map with a red pen marking the route she would have taken home along the river, across Kew Bridge to Brentford.

"Right, thanks for coming in tonight," began the DCI. "I know it's late, but this is an important case. DI Rob Miller will be heading up the investigation, so take your instruction from him. Twickenham Police has offered their assistance if we need more manpower, as well as surveillance teams from the Met's covert intelligence branch, should they be required."

Rob felt everybody's eyes on him and he knew they were all thinking the same thing.

Could he handle a case this size?

He bloody well hoped so, because this was his career break.

Lawrence nodded to Rob. "Over to you, Rob."

This was the second time he'd been Senior Investigating Officer. The first was a drunken brawl that had turned fatal when the victim had died in hospital, and the whole thing was caught on the CCTV cameras outside the pub. Apart from watching the grainy CCTV footage and charging the perpetrator, there hadn't been a lot of investigating involved.

This was a whole different ballgame.

"The victim is twenty-six-year-old Julie Andrews," he began, turning to point at the photograph of the victim behind him. He didn't know where Mallory had found the 'before' picture, but she looked beautiful in it. Her hair was loose, and the sun shone on her face as she smiled into the camera. She looked happy and full of life. He felt a surge of anger towards the man who had taken all that away from her. "She was walking home from work along the river towpath at Kew when she was attacked."

He outlined everything they knew of the attack, watching the collective expressions of outrage and disgust when he got to the sexual assault. "We don't know if it was pre or post-mortem yet, but the pathologist will clarify tomorrow."

There was a low murmur in the room. He held up a hand. "We're going to do whatever it takes to catch this bastard."

Nods all round.

"Now, I need a team on CCTV. I don't know what there is around the National Archives or along the river but see what you can find. Her route home is up here on the board. Make sure you look at previous days as well as today, I want to know if anyone was following her."

Three officers volunteered.

"Great, thanks guys."

Studying CCTV footage wasn't the most glamorous of jobs. They'd be shut away in a dark room for hours on end studying footage from tens if not hundreds of different cameras, but it was arguably one of the most important. In many cases he'd worked on, they'd managed to charge the perpetrator based solely on the video footage.

"Mallory is going to go to the victim's place of work tomorrow to question her colleagues." Mallory nodded.

"The rest of you, I want you to look into a report the victim filed a week or two ago regarding a possible stalker. Look at similar cases and see if you can find any similarities. This could be our first lead. I want to find something on this guy."

Heads nodded.

"Thanks everyone."

They filed out of the room talking amongst themselves. They'd do what they could tonight, then all be back first thing with renewed vigour.

"I've got the victim's boyfriend coming in tomorrow to give a statement," Rob told DCI Lawrence. "He wasn't in any state to do so tonight."

"Has he ID'ed the body?" asked Sam in his deep, gravelly voice. He was a massive, barrel-chested man in his fifties, about six four with a no-nonsense attitude and craggy face that wouldn't look amiss on a boxer, but it was his voice, more than anything else that commanded respect. It was deep, loud, and sounded like he'd smoked a million cigarettes then gargled with lighter fluid. If he hadn't been a policeman, he would have made an excellent movie-trailer voiceover artist.

"Becca's taken him to the mortuary tonight. He didn't want to wait."

"Just as well…" Sam scratched his bristly chin. "I don't have to tell you how big this is, Rob? The media are going to go berserk. A beautiful young girl like that raped and strangled on the Thames river path." He shook his head. "It's going to be shambolic."

"Will you give a statement?" asked Rob.

"No, but you will," confirmed Sam, with a grimace. "This is your case. I'll back you up if needs be."

Rob nodded. He hadn't dealt with the media before and had no idea what went into a press release. He'd seen it done, obviously, but hadn't paid much attention. Perhaps he'd better start.

"Vicky Bainbridge will help you," the DCI told him, as if reading his thoughts. "She's our press liaison officer. You can meet with her tomorrow morning."

"Okay, guv." Along with talking to Justin King, going to view the post-mortem and following up with everyone in the team. It was going to be a long day.

He stifled a yawn.

"Get yourself home," said Sam. "There's not much else you can do tonight. Start fresh in the morning."

"Yeah, okay."

He glanced at his watch. It was after two. Yvette would have turned in already.

Shit, her message. He quickly read it.

Thanks for letting me know you're okay. I'm going to bed. Make yourself comfortable on the couch.

She was pissed off, no doubt about it. He sighed, it couldn't be helped. She'd known what he did for a living when they'd first met. He'd never kept it a secret from her. In fact, he remembered telling her that he worked unsociable hours, sometimes for days on end. It had been okay back then, when they couldn't keep their hands off each other, but now, it seemed to annoy the hell out of her.

His thoughts turned to poor Julie, lying semi-naked in the bush, bruised and battered, and what she must have gone through in the moments before her death. The terror she must have experienced.

It was up to them to catch this murdering rapist and make him pay for what he'd done to her. He vowed that this crime would not go unpunished.

4

Yvette sulked all the way through breakfast, which consisted of a cup of coffee and a cigarette. She worked Tuesday to Saturday at Harrods in Knightsbridge, with Saturday being her longest and busiest day. Sunday and Monday were her weekend. That was the retail industry for you.

"I'm heading out now." Rob pulled on his jacket. Outside, it was cold and overcast. Spring had yet to kick in. "Don't wait up, I'll be late back."

Yvette shrugged, but didn't look at him.

He wondered if he ought to say something, try to explain about the case, about Julie, or how it was his responsibility to catch the killer, but he didn't. He wasn't sure why. Perhaps it was her stony expression or the lack of empathy she showed towards him, towards his job. All he knew was he didn't feel like labouring the point. Taking one last look at her petulant face, he sighed and walked out the door.

"I'VE GOT SOMETHING," said Celeste, a young female police officer who'd volunteered to trawl through the CCTV footage. She'd obviously been waiting for him, her cheeks pink with excitement. Rob felt a surge of adrenalin. That was quick. He dumped his rucksack on his desk and followed her into the studio where three large monitors were set up next to each other with CCTV video footage of varying quality playing on each.

"Where am I looking?" he asked.

"Here," she pointed to the third monitor that was frozen on a shadowy figure in a balaclava and a dark hoodie, lurking beside the trees in the Archive's grounds. "It's hard to see because he's so well camouflaged, but that's definitely someone watching her."

In the foreground, he could see the much lighter figure of Julie Andrews pausing outside the building. He scrutinized the screen. "It's impossible to see who he is from this shot. His face is covered and he's wearing a hoodie. He obviously knows what he's doing."

"I'll keep going, perhaps there's a shot of him without it further up the road."

"Hmm..." Rob was doubtful. Even if there was, unless he actually had the balaclava in his hand, it would be impossible to know if it was the same guy. Even the hoodie was black with no identifiable logos or markings that he could see. It wouldn't be enough. "Okay, thanks for that. Good work. Let me know if you find anything else."

Celeste took a seat in front of the monitor. "Will do, guv."

JUSTIN KING, Julie Andrews's boyfriend, was waiting in the interview room to give his statement. Rob sat down opposite him, the case file in front of him on the inhospitable metal table. Mallory was already there.

"Thanks for coming in," Rob began. "I know this is a difficult time for you."

Justin nodded. His eyes were red-rimmed and ringed with

dark shadows, and it didn't look like he'd shaved or brushed his hair. It was sticking up more so than yesterday, if that was possible. He was still in the same jeans, the same tracksuit top with the Nike tick on it.

"I want to help catch this bastard," he said.

"That's what we're going to do." Rob pressed a button on the electronic recording device. "Do you mind if we record this conversation?"

"Sure, if it'll help."

Rob opened the folder. "Justin, right now we want to try to piece together Julie's movements over the last week or so. If she was being followed, we might have a shot at identifying her stalker.

"So, you think he's the one who did this to her?"

"It's one line of enquiry," Rob said vaguely. At the moment it was their only line of enquiry. The shadowy guy in the CCTV footage could have been the stalker Julie described in the police report she'd filed three months ago, so it was definitely worth exploring.

"Okay, well she had the same routine every day. She left for work around eight in the morning – her hours were nine a.m. to five p.m. – and either took the bus to Kew or walked along the towpath, depending on the weather."

"Do you know which bus she took?" Mallory asked.

"I think it was the 65."

He made a note.

"What about after work?" asked Rob. "Did she always come home via the towpath?"

"Not always." Justin's voice quivered, and he stared down at his hands. "Yesterday was unusual, you see. We'd just got engaged and I was making a special supper to celebrate." He ended with a gut-wrenching sob and collapsed forwards onto the table.

There was a brief silence as his words sunk in. Rob was the

first to find his tongue. "I'm sorry, mate. That must be tough for you."

He could see Justin fighting to maintain control. Eventually, he sat back up, his eyes haunted.

"When did you get engaged?" Rob asked gently.

"Last weekend," said Justin desolately. "We went to pick out the ring together."

Ring?

Rob frowned, casting his mind back. "Would Julie have been wearing her engagement ring?"

"Yes, of course. Here, let me show you." He pulled his mobile phone out of his pocket and showed them a photograph from some social media site. It was of Julie's left hand, proudly showing off an elegant engagement ring comprising of a thin platinum band adorned with a single diamond. Probably one carat. Rob knew his guess was pretty accurate because he'd just bought something similar for Yvette, except hers had been one and a half carats and a thicker band. Yvette liked chunky jewellery.

Rob turned to Mallory. "The pathologist didn't mention a ring. Was it in evidence?"

Mallory shook his head. "No, we would have noticed. I went through everything." He frowned, and Rob knew he was worried he'd missed something. "But I'll double-check."

"Do you mind if we make a copy of this photograph?"

Justin shook his head. "Whatever helps."

Mallory held out his hand for the phone. "I'll do it."

Justin passed over the device and Mallory left the room.

"We didn't find a ring on the... on her finger," Rob explained. "So, either it fell off during the attack or her assailant took it."

"Do you think that's why she was targeted?" Justin's look was incredulous. "It wasn't even that big, I couldn't afford anything more than a carat."

"It's a possibility."

Justin shook his head. "But you're not convinced."

"No, given the nature of the attack, I think he'd been watching her for some time, waiting for his moment."

Justin closed his eyes. "I can't believe we didn't see this coming. The psycho had been following her for weeks and we just shrugged it off. We thought he'd disappeared, when all the time he was just biding his time."

"Did you manage to get a look at him?" asked Rob hopefully.

"No, I never saw him. It was only when Julie went out alone."

Rob turned the conversation back to Julie's routine. "So, she usually took the bus home, but last night she walked along the towpath?"

"It was quicker. The traffic at that time is crazy and the bus takes forever to cross Kew Bridge, so if it's not raining, she usually walks. Last night was an exception. Normally, she wouldn't walk in the rain, but she was eager to get home." He choked up again and Rob felt bad for making him relive the nightmare. "She texted me just before she left the office and said she was on her way. That's why I panicked when she wasn't home an hour later. I knew something awful had happened to her."

Rob made a note to check the time of Julie's text message. Her mobile phone had been found in her handbag along with her wallet containing the cash. It was still operational, which meant her attacker hadn't thought to turn it off. Or perhaps he'd known he wasn't going to be there long enough for anyone to trace her. Rob swallowed over the sour taste in his mouth. They'd applied for her phone records, which were being sent over.

"Okay, this was her daily routine. What about weekends? Did she go out without you last weekend?"

"Hang on, let me think." Justin rubbed his forehead. "I proposed on Friday night and we went ring shopping on Saturday morning. We had lunch in Richmond then came home and as far as I can remember, we didn't go out again.

On Sunday, Julie had coffee with a friend." He clicked his fingers. "She went out alone, because they met at a café in Chiswick."

"Friend's name?" asked Rob.

"Natasha," said Justin. "I'm afraid I don't know her surname. She used to work with Julie at the Archives but left some time ago and they've kept in touch."

Rob made another note for Mallory to follow that up when he went over to the archives.

He tried to push Justin about events the weekend before, but he couldn't remember it in any great detail. They'd gone to watch the football at the local pub, The Waterman's Arms, on Saturday afternoon, he knew that much, and he hadn't gone anywhere on Sunday. Julie may have popped to the local grocery store, but he couldn't be sure what time.

Rob called it quits after that. They had quite a bit to follow up on. He only hoped it was enough. It would be an extremely lucky break if they could catch a clearer glimpse of Julie's stalker on one of the CCTV cameras in the area. Her phone records would also give them a better idea of where she'd been and what she'd been up to.

Mallory came back in and returned Justin's phone to him. "Thanks mate, that's extremely useful." He glanced at Rob. "Definitely no ring."

Justin pocketed it, then looked Rob in the eye. "Please, you've got to find this guy. He needs to pay for what he did to my Julie."

Rob held his gaze. "I intend to."

"WHAT HAVE you got for me on the stalker's M.O.?" Rob directed his question to Will Freemont and Jenny Bird, two experienced sergeants who were working on that angle. Will cleared his throat. "Julie Andrews did report him ten days ago. She came in to Richmond Station and spoke to the duty officer. He took a full statement."

"Good, and what did you find on him?"

"Not a lot, to be honest. She gave a vague description, tall, lanky with thin face, wearing a hoodie."

"Matches the guy we've got on CCTV following her down to the river last night," he said. "Anything specific about his appearance, or his features?"

"Nothing that will help to identify him, guv. She never really got a good look at his face, it was always in shadow."

"But she was sure it was the same guy?"

"According to her statement, she was adamant. She said she'd noticed him three or four times already, outside her home in Brentford, at the supermarket, on her way to work…"

"Did you say supermarket?"

Will glanced down at his notes. "Sainsbury's."

"Her fiancé mentioned something about Julie going to the supermarket the weekend before last. Let's see if we can find some CCTV on that? Sainsbury's is bound to have cameras outside the store, particularly in the carpark."

"On it, guv."

It was a start. If only they could get an ID on this guy. He checked his watch. The post-mortem was scheduled for twelve noon.

"I'd better get down to the mortuary," he told Mallory, who was also getting ready to leave. "Did you get my message about her friend, Natasha?"

"Yeah, the one that left. I'll get her details from HR and follow up."

They parted ways in the police carpark.

Rob drove to the Fulham Public Mortuary where Julie's body was being kept.

The forensic pathologist introduced himself as Robert Gowan

and once Rob had scrubbed up, he began the procedure. The only other people in the room were the two trainee pathologists who were assisting, but judging by their calm, professional demeanours, they'd done this before. Rob stood a few metres away from the body, watching silently. This wasn't his first autopsy, but he still felt queasy as he stared at the discoloured corpse on the steel table in front of him. It was unrecognizable as the beautiful, happy woman whose photo was stuck on the incident room white-board.

"You okay?" Gowan paused. "You've gone awfully pale."

"I'm good." Rob averted his eyes, focusing on the array of sterile equipment positioned around the edge of the room. Anything to replace the bloated, mottled remains of Julie Andrews. It wasn't essential he watch every detail of the post-mortem, but if there was anything to be found, he wanted to know now, not in a week's time when the report landed on his desk.

"The victim is a well-nourished white female twenty-six years of age, previously identified as Julie Andrews," said Gowan inspecting the body.

Rob took a deep, steadying breath. He desperately needed something on this guy, and he was hoping against hope that Julie's body would offer that something up. A sliver of DNA would do the trick. A piece of skin under her fingernails, or a hint of semen in her vagina.

"There are deep bruises around her neck and petechia on the face and conjunctiva indicative of asphyxiation." He looked up. "In other words, she was strangled."

"Was that the cause of death?"

"Yes. She has congealed blood in her nasal passages and her nose is swollen, which is consistent with a punch to the face. While the swelling is severe, I don't think this is what killed her."

The pathologist worked his way down her body, pointing out

all the defensive wounds where she'd lashed out at her attacker, or tried to fight him off.

"Anything under her fingernails?" Rob knew it was a long shot.

"Not that I can see." He held her hand gently and scraped beneath her nails with a sterile instrument, which he then passed to one of his assistants who transferred the sample to a test-tube for lab analysis. He repeated the process with every finger. "I'm taking samples, just in case."

Rob sighed.

When he was done, he turned her wrists over and inspected the markings through an illuminated magnifying glass on a stretchy arm that allowed for 360-degree motion. "Her hands were bound as is evident by the deep striations and bruising around her wrists."

"There is evidence of sexual assault," he said grimly, coming to the bottom half of her body. "Inflammation and bruising caused by penetration." He peered in closer, pulling the magnifying glass with him. "No evidence of semen present in the vagina."

Shit.

Rob ground his teeth. The guy must have worn a condom.

One of the assistants handed him a metal device which he inserted and opened to gain access to the vagina. Then he used what looked like a cotton bud on a long stick to collect a sample. "I've taken a swab to be sure, but the results won't be back for a few days."

"Thanks." Rob got ready to leave. He'd seen all he needed to see, and he definitely didn't want to be around when he sliced her open.

"Wait a minute," barked the pathologist without looking up.

Rob froze. "What is it?"

A pause, then he said, "I've found something wedged inside her vagina."

Rob's pulse rate increased. Was it the condom? Had it come off and got lodged inside her? He found he was holding his breath.

"Forceps," snapped Gowan. An assistant handed them over. He gently inserted them and retrieved the object.

"It's a ring." The surprise was evident on his face, as he studied it under the magnifying glass.

"A ring?" Rob moved closer in order to have a better look. "What kind of ring?"

The doctor dropped it into a metallic kidney-bowl with a metallic clunk and thrust it under his nose. "It looks like a diamond ring."

Rob stared at it. "Fucking hell. It's her engagement ring."

"I've seen a thing or two in my time," said Dr. Gowan, "but I have to admit, this is a first."

"CAN I HAVE YOUR ATTENTION, PLEASE?" DCI Sam Lawrence had barely raised his voice, yet everyone immediately stopped what they were doing and turned to face him. They were in the squad room, the blinds were drawn to keep the sunlight off the monitor screens, and the stuffy atmosphere bristled with anticipation.

"We have a new development. Rob, do you want to do the honours?"

Rob looked at the faces of his team looking back at him. He got straight to it. "During the post mortem, the pathologist discovered a ring wedged up inside the victim."

There were a few horrified gasps and a quiet murmur.

"I know, it is shocking, but this puts a different spin on things. We are now looking for a man who has a deep-seated grudge against this woman. This was personal. So, I want you to look into her past associates, ex-boyfriends, anyone who might have resented her relationship with Justin King."

"What about his ex-girlfriends?" asked Jenny Bird from the back of the room.

"Yes, good point," said Rob, who'd been getting to that. "We're going to need to talk to Justin King again."

"We've decided to keep this back from the press," interjected the DCI in his gravelly voice. "For now." He turned so he could survey everyone in the room. "If anything about a ring turns up in *The Daily Mail* tomorrow, I'll know it was one of you lot. So, mum's the word. Is that clear?"

They all nodded.

Rob cleared his throat. "Mallory has an update from Julie's workplace." He nodded to Mallory who stood up.

"Yeah, I interviewed her colleagues today and she did mention a stalker. Two of the women in her office clearly remember her telling them about him about two weeks ago. We don't have a description unfortunately, other than a tall, creepy guy in a hoodie, but at least this backs up the police report and the guy we saw on CCTV outside the archives the day she was murdered."

"What about the friend? The one she met for lunch?" asked Rob.

"Natasha Wakefield. Julie met her for lunch in Chiswick last Sunday. They went to Annie's restaurant on Thames Road."

"Right," said Rob, directing his voice to Celeste and the other two detectives covering the CCTV footage. "Can we look for any evidence of a tall, creepy man in a hoodie following her in Chiswick, please? We really need to get a decent shot of this guy. If he's been stalking her as regularly as it seems, he should be easy enough to spot on some camera somewhere."

"We think we may have the stalker outside her flat earlier in the week," Celeste replied, standing on her toes so she could see him above the heads of the others. "I was about to come and find you," she added, when she saw his face.

"I'm on my way," he barked. "Thanks guys, that's it for now."

"Don't forget the press conference in an hour." DCI Lawrence smiled thinly. "Have you spoken to Vicky yet?"

"Not yet." Rob wondered where he was supposed to find the time. He'd just have to wing it. How hard could a press statement be?

"I'll get her down here," said Lawrence, who was having none of it. "Meet me in my office in ten minutes." His tone didn't warrant arguing with.

Rob marched through to the video studio. "Can I see it?"

Celeste nodded to the screen on the right. "The timestamp is seven fifty-three Wednesday morning before Julie leaves for work." Rob watched as a dark figure in the signature hoodie appeared in the bottom left corner of the screen. The shot was from the back, but he looked to be peering through the steel security fencing that surrounded the apartment where Julie lived with her fiancé.

"He's waiting for her to leave," said Celeste.

"Turn around," Rob muttered to the figure on the screen.

"There's Julie." Celeste pointed to the screen as a petite brunette walked out of the front entrance and turned right towards Kew Bridge. She appeared much smaller in the video than she had lying in the bushes. Five foot four, the pathologist had said. A big man like the stalker would have no trouble subduing her. Rob pictured the bruises on her slender neck and then looked at the stalker's hands. *Easy.*

Julie didn't notice the man watching her, nor did she see him following her as she walked across the bridge. He stayed at least a hundred metres behind her and kept to the opposite side of the bridge, invisible amongst the morning crowd. He made sure to keep his face angled downwards, so it was always in shadow.

"Shit, we still can't get an ID on him." Rob was getting frustrated. "This guy knows what he's doing."

He watched them until they disappeared off the screen.

"Then what?" he asked Celeste.

She sighed. "The next camera is at the wrong angle, and the one after that only covers her side of the bridge."

"What about the river path?"

"Nothing on there until you get to the Old Ship, which is past the path leading to the Archives."

Rob reigned in his disappointment. "Okay, thanks." As an afterthought, he added, "Good work, Celeste. We're getting closer."

It was essential to keep morale up. He'd been part of murder squads before where the SIO had got grumpy and frustrated, and it put a damper on the whole team. He wanted his team alert and motivated.

DCI Lawrence was waiting in his office with the press officer, Vicky Bainbridge, as promised. Rob had noticed Vicky around, but they'd never met. She was an attractive woman in her thirties, dressed like she'd stepped out of a magazine article on power-dressing in the boardroom. Her dark hair was scraped back into a no-nonsense bun and her make-up was meticulously applied, right down to the strawberry-coloured gloss that coated her lips. Everything about her screamed marketability and efficiency. She had a lovely smile, though, and enormous brown eyes that gave him a thorough once-over as he walked through the door.

"Anything on the CCTV?" Lawrence asked before Rob could say hello.

"Nope, not yet." He didn't go into detail. When they had something definite, then he'd let the DCI know.

"Okay, now I know this is your first press conference, so Vicky here is going to go through it with you. There are certain things we can and can't say. Impartiality and integrity, and all that."

Rob smiled at Vicky and held out his hand. "Rob Miller," he said.

"Vicky Bainbridge, press liaison." She ate him up with her eyes.

Rob was momentarily thrown. It had been a while since anyone had looked at him like that. It wasn't that he was interested, just flattered. All Yvette seemed to do was scowl at him these days.

Rob tried to stay focused as she began to outline the important aspects of giving a press statement. Dealing with the media was not his forte. He knew it was an important part of the job, and the higher you got in the force, the more you had to do it, but right now he was preoccupied with catching a killer.

They went through it for the remainder of the hour, and contrary to what he'd thought going in, he felt a lot more confident about addressing the media going out.

"I'll take you downstairs," said Vicky. "They're waiting for you outside."

He shot a look at his DCI.

"I'll be there too," Lawrence said. "To make sure you don't fuck up."

"Good Afternoon, Ladies and Gentlemen. My name is Detective Inspector Rob Miller and I'm the Senior Investigating Officer on this case. The body of a local woman was discovered on the river towpath near Kew shortly after six-thirty last night. I can now confirm that her name was Julie Andrews, aged twenty-six, from Brentford. It is believed she was walking home from work when she was attacked."

"Was there any sign of sexual assault?" A female journalist in the front row jumped the gun. Rob was always amazed at how quickly news got around.

He glanced at DCI Lawrence who gave a barely discernible nod.

"Yes, she was raped and strangled."

A ripple went through the group, then they all started talking at once.

"Do you know who the rapist was?"

"How close are you to apprehending the murderer?"

"Do you have any suspects?"

"Should we be worried? Is there a serial killer on the loose?"

Rob felt like a deer in headlights, but he somehow managed to maintain his composure. He lifted his hand and did what he'd seen DCI Lawrence do on several occasions. Raise his voice and talk over everyone. "We are currently pursuing all avenues of enquiry. That's it for now. Thank you."

"Christ, did you hear that question about a serial killer?" DCI Lawrence said stony-faced as they marched back upstairs. "That's all we bloody need."

"Given the nature of the attack and where we found the ring, it's more likely to be personal," said Rob. "A once-off."

Vicky nodded in agreement. "I'd put my money on a jealous ex-boyfriend."

"I hope to God you're right," said Lawrence heading straight for his office. "Keep me updated, Rob."

"Good job, by the way." Vicky paused outside the incident room. "That wasn't bad for your first press conference."

"I kept it short and sweet." Rob smiled at her. "Just like you said."

She chuckled and gave him a flirtatious look. "You're a fast learner, DI Miller. I like that in a man." And she disappeared down the corridor to her office.

5

Rob left work at six and went via Julie Andrews' apartment to talk to her fiancé again. He'd called ahead so Justin was expecting him.

"I'm sorry to bother you again," he began, "But we're following a certain line of enquiry and I wanted to ask you some more questions. Would that be okay?"

Justin nodded and sat down in a well-worn armchair. The TV remote lay on the scuffed but sturdy coffee table, along with a cup of coffee that, judging by the layer of congealed milk on top, looked like it might have been there for some time. He gestured for Rob to take a seat.

Easing his tall frame onto a leather sofa, he organised his thoughts. "We wanted to ask you if you knew of anyone who might want to harm Julie?"

Justin's eyes widened, and he blinked several times before replying. "No, of course not. Everybody loved Julie. She was a great girl. Why do you ask?"

"Like I said, it's just a line of enquiry. What about ex-boyfriends or anyone she may have dated in the past?"

"We've been together for two years," Justin said, causing Rob's heart to sink. "As far as I know she hasn't kept in touch with anyone she dated before that."

"What about on social media?" He was grasping at straws here.

"I don't know." Justin hung his head. "Maybe."

"Okay, not to worry." He already had someone working on her social media profiles, looking for evidence of harassment or aggressive behaviour. "What about you? Any ex-girlfriends who might be upset that you'd got engaged to Julie?"

"What? No. Nothing like that." He frowned. "Like I said, we'd been together for two years. Before that I was at university up in Edinburgh and there was no one serious."

Rob sighed. Another dead end. So much for the jealous ex theory.

He thanked Justin, apologised again for intruding and was about to leave when a thought struck him. "Hey, do you have security cameras in this building?"

Justin gave him a vacant look. "I don't know. It's possible. You'd have to speak to the management company."

"You got their details?"

Justin nodded and got up. "Gimme a sec." He came back five minutes later with a letter about residents parking which he handed to Rob. "It's on that." He pointed to the top. "You can keep it."

Rob thanked him again and left. On the way to his car he took a good look at the security set-up around the building. There was a camera positioned above the front entrance, just outside the lobby. It was pointing downwards so it would pick up whoever was buzzing for entry. It wouldn't pick up anyone standing outside the perimeter. He strolled around the corner and looked up. Bingo. At first floor level, another camera pointed towards the gate. The stalker had been standing about twenty-metres to the left of the gate, so it may well have picked him up.

Encouraged, Rob walked out through the gates, checking the mechanism as he did so. There was no automatic apparatus, which meant they were probably open permanently. He turned back to survey the apartment block. To the right of the gate was steel fencing, through which the stalker had been watching. It ran for almost a full city block, past the Brentford water tower, all the way to the traffic intersection. On the other side, was a six-foot brick wall which continued to where the shops on the High Street began. There were lots of vantage points if you wanted to survey the building. Hell, the stalker could even have driven in and parked his car in one of the visitor's bays while he waited for Julie to appear. He flicked the paper containing the management company's number. First thing tomorrow he'd get hold of them and request any footage they had. There was still a chance they could identify the guy from that.

Yvette was out when Rob got home. He wasn't surprised, it was Saturday night and she liked to unwind after her Saturday shift ended. Sometimes, she went clubbing with a bunch of workmates. In the beginning, she used to invite him, but he always declined, clubbing wasn't his thing. He had no natural rhythm and couldn't see the point of dancing all night without talking. The music was always too loud for any meaningful conversation. Give him a pub over a club any day. She didn't bother anymore.

Rob had a shower and made himself a sandwich, then took a beer out of the fridge and sat down in his favourite armchair to eat and think. He was still sitting there two hours later when Yvette got home. He knew she was drunk before she'd even come into the house, given how many times it took her to get her key into the lock. Then she'd stumbled past the lounge, seen the light on and poked her head around the door.

"Oh, what a surprise," she laughed scornfully. "You home before me."

He got up and moved towards her.

"I saw you on television tonight," she said. Her eyes were glazed and off-focus. "You never told me about that girl who was raped and murdered."

"I haven't had a chance to," he said.

"Everybody was asking me about it tonight and I couldn't tell them anything because I didn't know." She tottered on her heels. "The first I heard was on the TV."

"I would have told you," he said putting an arm around her waist. "As soon as we had a chance to talk."

"Talk?" She laughed again. "You have to spend time with someone to talk to them."

"I know. Listen, this case is a big one. Once it's over, we'll spend some quality time together. I promise."

She raised a perfectly plucked eyebrow and turned to go upstairs. "I'm tired. I wanna go to bed."

He tried to help her up the stairs, but she shrugged him off. "I'm okay." She clearly wasn't, but he wisely kept his mouth shut.

While she got ready for bed, he locked up and turned off all the lights. When he got upstairs, she'd collapsed on the duvet and was fast asleep.

He climbed in next to her, but she didn't stir. It always amazed him that no matter how inebriated she got, she always managed to take her make-up off before falling into bed. He gazed at her freshly-scrubbed face and marvelled at her model bone structure, clear skin and long, dark eyelashes. She was a beautiful woman and when she was in a good mood, she made the world seem so much brighter. Unfortunately, that didn't seem to be very often these days.

She slept on her stomach, the oversized T-shirt she wore to bed riding up around her waist, displaying long, tanned legs and a perfectly shaped derrière, as she called it. There was a reason she'd been a lingerie model. He'd never met anyone with a body to rival hers. After the day he'd had, he longed to take her in his arms and make love to her, wipe out the image of Julie lying on the slab, the horror of her murder and the sickness of the man they were trying to find, but he knew she wouldn't be forthcoming. He'd have to live with his demons for a while longer. So, he turned over, switched off the bedside lamp and tried to fall sleep.

THE STALKER WATCHED as a young woman left a house in Queens Road in her running gear. She was a new target and he was still getting to know her. He felt nervous and excited at the same time, like he always did in the beginning stages of a new project. Julie had been a long time in coming. He'd planned it meticulously and executed it perfectly, but it had made him hungry for more. So here he was, upping his schedule. A hunter, scouting out his prey, looking for weakness, for opportunity.

He watched as she jogged at an easy pace up the road, her dark pony-tail bobbing as she moved. Sara, her name was, he'd seen it on the mailing list sign-up form.

Well, Sara, what do you like doing in your free time? Where do you hang out?

Soon, he would know it all.

A keen jogger, she ran through Richmond Park every evening around six-thirty. The park was closed to motorists at that time given that the sun had already set, but it was still light enough to determine the gravel path around the perimeter. To assist her, she wore a light attached to an elastic band around her forehead and a high visibility jacket.

Given the upmarket three-storey Victorian townhouse she lived in and her expensive running gear, she had chosen well. Her fiancé worked in the city and drove a Porsche Cayenne Turbo, which retailed at about a hundred thousand pounds. Right now, it was parked in their ample driveway, alongside her factory-fresh Mini Cooper. Not bad for a mixed-race girl from Peterborough.

She was pretty, though, with a firm body and bouncy breasts, but all money-grabbing whores were. That's how they managed to secure rich husbands.

He got out of his vehicle and spat on the ground. She'd pay, just like the others.

He followed her on foot, keeping to the shadows. He lived in the shadows, he wasn't the kind of man people noticed. When he was younger, he'd wished it was different, but that's before he'd realised his true calling. Now, he used those skills to his advantage. A predator needed to blend in, until the time was right to strike.

When she turned through the gates into Richmond Park, he stopped. There was no need to follow her in.

Not tonight.

He backtracked to a pub called the Lass O' Richmond Hill and went inside. It wasn't busy, and he bought a pint of cider and sat at a table by the window facing the street. From here, he would be able to see her when she returned. The stopwatch on his phone was on, counting the minutes until she came back.

AT FOUR IN the morning Rob felt Yvette's arms around him and her lips on his mouth. At first, he thought he was dreaming but then as his body woke up and began to respond, he knew he wasn't. They made love quietly, but with a sense of urgency, and when they were done, Yvette lay panting in his arms.

"I miss you when you're not here," she sulked.

"I know and I'm sorry. I'll make it up to you after we catch this guy."

"The rapist?"

"Yeah."

"Was it bad?" she asked hesitantly. "Did you see her body?"

"I did, and it was bad." He gently stroked her hair, not wanting to upset her with the gory details.

"How horrible." She shuddered then rolled over taking his arm with her. He turned onto his side and spooned her for a while. He could tell by her breathing when she'd gone back to sleep.

Not so for him.

After twenty minutes of lying in the dark, he decided to get up and walk to work. It was Sunday, so the streets would be quiet, and Yvette would probably want to sleep off her hangover, anyway.

The station was deserted when he arrived. He walked through the darkened corridors up to the squad room, watching the fluorescent lights flicker to life as his body movement activated the sensors. Once settled, he pulled up the report Julie Andrews had lodged almost two weeks ago. He read through it carefully, then made a note of the duty officer who'd taken her statement. It might be worth giving him a buzz.

Next, he took a look at Julie's phone records that Will Freeman had been working on. The text message she'd sent Justin King before she'd left the office was there, highlighted on the screen. There was nothing after that. No incoming or outgoing calls.

He got a cup of coffee from the machine in the hall – Starbucks hadn't been open when he'd arrived – and went back to his desk. People started arriving and by eight-thirty telephones were ringing and the room was buzzing. It might be Sunday, but for them, it was just another day at the office.

At five past nine he rang the management company at Justin King's block of flats. Nobody answered. He tried again at quarter past. Same thing. Perhaps they didn't work on Sundays? Then, he dialled the duty officer's number, but he didn't pick up either. It was his work desk, and he should be in by now. Annoyed, Rob decided to go and hunt him down. He took the stairs and went down two floors to the uniformed division. "I'm looking for Andrew Collins," he told the guy at the front desk.

"Along the passage, second door to your right."

"Cheers." He pushed open the second door to the right and found himself in an open-plan office with a massive overhead projector screen at one end and a small kitchenette at the other. There were a handful of officers hanging around drinking coffee and waiting for their shifts to start, or end.

"Andrew Collins?" he asked the first guy he saw.

"Andy." He gestured to a young guy with flaming red hair.

"Yeah?" Andy came over.

"Don't you answer your phone?" barked Rob.

"I've just got in," he said, stating the obvious. "What can I do for you?"

"I'm DI Rob Miller from upstairs." Even though they worked in the same building, they didn't all know each other, and Rob didn't think he'd seen PC Andrew Collins before. "I'm SIO on the Julie Andrews case and I read that you're the guy who logged her report on the stalker a couple of weeks back."

Collins puffed out his chest. It wasn't often they got a visit from the plainclothes guys upstairs. "Yes, that was me. She was in a right state. Said the guy had followed her all the way into town."

"Wait. You mean the stalker actually followed her into Richmond?"

"Yeah, I guess so. She was here for hours, she didn't want to leave. Then, when she did, she called a cab. I think the guy totally freaked her out." He shook his head. "Who would have thought he'd get her in the end, hey?"

"*We* should have thought of that," snapped Rob, who was fast losing his temper. "Then maybe she'd still be alive today."

The PC shuffled uncomfortably. His mate, the first guy Rob had spoken to stood nearby pretending he wasn't listening, but was in fact, all ears.

"What time did she come in?" asked Rob.

"Isn't it on the report?"

"No, you've just put the date, not the time. If I want to check CCTV in Richmond, I'm going to need an approximate time."

The PC thought for a moment. "Well, it was before my lunch break, so I'd say around eleven. It was a Saturday, I remember that much, 'cos I always get the weekend shift."

"Yes, thank you. I knew that from the report."

Then he turned and marched out, leaving the guy standing there staring after him.

"They're always like that, upstairs," his friend said. "Think they own the bloody place."

6

Rob was impressed that his entire team had made it into work. Motivation was high, and he was pleased to see heads down, people on phones, and a general buzz of determination in the air. The first thing Rob did when he got back from talking to PC Collins, was call a briefing in the incident room.

"I've just found out that Julie's stalker followed her into Richmond town centre on the twenty-third of March. Apparently, she was so freaked out she came straight here and lodged a complaint against him. Now, we don't know how she got here, but she doesn't have a car, so it would have been public transport. I need at least three more people on CCTV checking all the bus and train routes from Brentford to Richmond that morning."

When no one immediately put up their hands, Rob looked around. "I'm going to nominate you, you and you." He chose two male sergeants and one female constable who were standing together in a clump.

They all nodded. With DCI Lawrence standing beside Rob, no one would dare refuse.

"Good. Now PC Collins, the duty officer who took her statement, said Julie came in about eleven o'clock on the twenty-third. Let's check her route before and after that time. He must be somewhere. Come on, guys. This is how we're going to catch this guy."

DCI Lawrence asked, "Anything on her social media profiles?"

"No, sir," said Jenny, who'd been assigned that task. "She had less than a hundred Facebook friends and they all check out. Her privacy settings were on high, so only her friends could see her profile, and she had no new friends and no one sending her threatening or suggestive messages. She was on Instagram but hadn't used it in some time and had no other social media accounts."

DCI Lawrence grimaced and gave a curt nod.

"Where are we on the CCTV at that restaurant in Chiswick?" Rob asked Celeste. She shook her head, making her short brown curls bounce. "The only camera in the street showed Julie arriving on foot, but there was no one matching our stalker's description either before or after her. I checked an hour each way."

"The guy's a ghost," muttered one of the young constables at the front of the room.

"I assure you it wasn't a ghost who raped and strangled Julie Andrews," said Rob, giving him an icy stare. The guy dropped his gaze and flushed.

"He's out there, people. Let's find him. He can't be invisible."

"One more thing," barked DCI Lawrence as Rob finished up the meeting. All heads turned back to the front. "The press has set up camp across the road, so when you go out, use the fire escape at the back of the building. We're the only murder team working today, so they're likely to bombard any and all of you with questions about the investigation."

There were murmurs of consent and some of excitement. For many officers here, this was their first big case and the interest of the national press made it feel even bigger. For Rob, that meant more pressure.

Back at his desk, he tried the management company again. No luck. They probably didn't work weekends. God forbid there was a problem at the premises. The place could burn down and they wouldn't know till Monday morning when someone got in and bothered to pick up the phone.

"Rob, a word." DCI Lawrence poked his head around his glass office door.

"I'm getting heat from Scotland Yard," he began, pacing around his office. He was clearly agitated, which Rob knew from experience was never a good sign.

"What kind of heat?"

"They want to send in their top murder investigation team to assist us, which basically means take over the investigation."

"It's only the second day," said Rob, a sinking feeling in his gut. His career breaking case and he might not get to see out the week.

"I know, and I've convinced them to give us a few more days, but if we don't have a firm lead by then, we're going to have to roll over."

"Shit."

"Exactly. So, find me something I can give them, Rob. DNA, an ID, anything to help us get this guy."

"I'm doing my best." Rob felt like his back was up against the wall. "This guy's a pro. He knows how to avoid the cameras. I've got six people working on CCTV and they can't find him."

"Double it," snapped Lawrence. "And let's put out a public appeal."

"Really?" Rob wasn't questioning his DCI's judgement, he was just conscious of creating mass panic. The press was salivating downstairs as it was.

"Yeah, we're fucking desperate. Someone must have seen something."

"Okay, I'll speak to them."

"Take Mallory with you," said Lawrence wryly. "There's safety in numbers."

Rob scoffed. "Thanks."

He made to leave, but then turned and asked, "Who's in charge of the Yard's MIT? Anyone we know?"

"No. It's some sparkling new DCI from Manchester who transferred down a few months ago. She has an excellent arrest record and of course she ticks all the right boxes. The Commissioner loves her."

"Oh, that's just great." He was going to lose his career case to the Commissioner's pet. Brilliant.

He turned to leave the office.

"Find me something, Rob," Lawrence called after him. "And find it fast."

The day continued in the same frenzied manner in which it had begun. The coffee machine worked overtime and because the press was lurking outside, Rob ordered pizza for lunch, which he put on the department's budget. The team fell on it like starving hyenas. With almost half the squad working the CCTV angle, he'd given the other half the task of following up on any old stalking, rape and strangulation cases – anything that might suggest the crimes were carried out by the same guy. Rob figured if he was this good, he must have had practise.

After grabbing a reluctant Mallory, he went downstairs and much to the media's excitement, issued a public appeal for information. He gave them the only description he could: tall, lanky man in a dark hoodie with a thin face. It wasn't much to go on, but like the DCI had said, someone may have seen something. It would go out on the six o'clock news.

Then he called Twickenham police station who would be handling the calls. "Anything in the vicinity of Kew Retail Park or the National Archives on the night of the murder is of particular significance," he told them. He gave them the other dates Justin King had given him, and of course, Julie's trip to Richmond Police Station on the twenty-third.

At six, he turned on the news. The appeal went out as planned. It felt weird seeing himself on TV, almost like he was watching an efficient, more professional version of himself. His hair was in place, his jacket buttoned up and he even managed to sound calm and composed with the right sense of urgency. He wondered if Yvette had seen it.

Please let someone have seen something, he prayed. Then his phone rang.

"DI Miller." He didn't glance at the number, his eyes still on the flatscreen TV.

"Rob, it's Tony. I've just seen you on the telly. Going up in the world, mate?"

Rob drew his eyes away and smiled into his mobile.

"Something like that. Thanks for returning my call. Listen, mate, I need to pick your brain. Are you free tonight?"

"The stalker case, huh?"

"How did you guess?"

Tony laughed, a deep resonance that stemmed from his belly. He'd always had a great laugh.

"My son's playing in a football tournament today, but I can meet you at eight. Will that do?"

"Perfect, how about The Cricketers?" The pub on Richmond Green was the go-to place for cricket fans and those who turned up to watch the local team play on the green on summery Saturday afternoons. Out of season it was a quiet and convenient place in which to talk.

"I'll be there."

"First let's look at the what, and why of the crime, then we can concentrate on the who," said Tony, after they'd got the pleasantries out the way.

It was great seeing his old mate again. Tony looked well, fit and healthy, with ample laughter lines that spoke of a happy relationship. He had two kids now, he told Rob, and Kim, his wife, had just gone back to work as a nurse in their local NHS Trust hospital. It all seemed very domestic and Rob was hit by a pang of envy for Tony's comfortable, happy life. Yvette might be a stunner with a body that made most men stare at him in awe, but she had made it quite clear she didn't want children. They'd had that discussion when they were dating, before he'd proposed. She'd felt it important he know up front. It was non-negotiable. Rob hadn't given kids much thought and with his career on the rise, he didn't think it would be a problem. But now, listening to Tony go on about his ten-year-old, playing football with him on weekends and taking him to the Arsenal games, he suddenly wasn't so sure.

He forced his attention back to the case. "The what, and the why?"

"Yes, if I was going to profile your killer, I'd have to know what crime he committed and why it was done. For example, what was behaviourally significant about the crime, why did it happen the way it did? Based on that, I could hazard a guess about the kind of person who would have committed this crime for these reasons."

"Hazard a guess?" said Rob. "I was hoping for a bit more than that."

Tony laughed again.

"It's all elaborate guesswork at the end of the day, but it's pretty efficient. There are patterns that we see in most offenders, but we'll come to that later."

Rob took a swig of his beer. It tasted like manna from heaven after the bitter machine coffee he'd been chugging back all day. "The victim was Julie Andrews. She was twenty-six and she worked at the National Archives in Kew. She was attacked on her way home, pulled into the bushes, raped and then strangled."

Tony didn't react. "How was she raped? Was she tied in a specific way? Was anything taken? Was she strangled before or after she was molested?"

The questions came fast and furious and Rob was glad he'd suggested meeting up tonight.

"Her hands were tied above her head with duct-tape and also around a small tree trunk. She had another piece of tape over her mouth." Rob cast his mind back to the rainy river path. "She had bruises around her wrists where she'd struggled against the bindings. The pathologist said she must have put up a fight."

"Which would have made it difficult for the stalker," said Tony. "How did he subdue her long enough to tie her up?"

Rob raised an eyebrow. "You're good at this shit, Tony."

"I should hope so, since it's my job."

Rob pictured the victim's battered face and frowned. "She had a bloody nose. We think he hit her in the face."

Tony nodded. "Makes sense."

His frown deepened. "Then, he raped and strangled her, possibly at the same time, but she died from asphyxiation."

"Anything else?" asked Tony, when Rob reached for his drink. He suddenly felt dirty, like he needed to take a shower. He took a big gulp, hoping to wash the sensation away.

"Well, she'd reported a stalker three weeks earlier, but nothing was done about it. She filed a report with a rough description. Tall, thin, wearing a hoodie."

"Yeah, I saw that on the news."

"What does it mean? Why did this guy target her? Was it a personal vendetta or something?"

Tony studied him. "What makes you think it's personal?"

"Well, the intimate manner in which she was attacked and the ring." He stopped. Shit, he wasn't supposed to mention the ring.

"What ring?" Tony jumped on it.

"I can't say." Rob bit his lip. "Sorry, strict orders from above."

"The ring is significant," said Tony. "Was it missing?"

"Not exactly." Rob shifted uncomfortably in his chair. Lawrence would kill him when he found out... "This can't go any further, okay?"

Tony nodded.

"It was found inside the victim's body."

Tony stared at him. A full minute passed without either of them saying anything at all. Finally, Tony broke the silence. His voice was a whisper. "What kind of ring was it?"

Rob exhaled. "You know, I could get into serious shit if this came out?"

"It won't go any further than this pub," Tony reassured him. "Listen, if you want my help, you need to tell me about the ring."

"It was an engagement ring," he breathed, his eyes darting around the pub to make sure no one was listening. All the other drinkers were minding their own business.

Tony blinked as Rob's words sunk in, then he muttered, "She was engaged."

"Yeah?"

"That's it."

"That's what?"

Tony leaned forward. "It was the fact that she was engaged that made him select her."

Rob tried to think. "Are you saying this wasn't a personal attack on Julie Andrews? That it was because she was engaged that she was attacked?"

Tony sat back in his chair and picked up his drink. "That's exactly what I'm saying."

"But he was stalking her for weeks before he attacked her. That must mean something?"

"Sure, it means he picked her out as his next target and

followed her until he knew her routine, then he waited for the right opportunity to grab her."

Rob felt ill. "What do you mean his next target? Do you think he's done this sort of thing before?"

"Oh, almost certainly," said Tony. "And I'll tell you something else for free. She won't be the last either."

THE BLOODY JOURNALIST WAS RIGHT. "He's a serial killer."

His voice was strained as if the tension he'd been holding in his neck and shoulders had suddenly risen to his throat and gripped his voice-box. He had another large swig. It helped dislodge the lump.

"It looks like it." Tony wasn't smiling now.

Rob stared at his friend over his pint glass. "And you figured all this out based on the ring?"

"Let me tell you about the patterns."

Tony dropped his voice as a group of four occupied the table next to them. "You probably know some, if not all of this already, but bear with me."

Rob nodded and slid his glass onto the table. He was picturing DCI Lawrence's face when he told him they had a freaking serial murderer on their hands.

"He probably started with some basic stalking. Perhaps he liked a girl who didn't like him back, perhaps he hit on her and she rejected him, that sort of thing. It's possible she then got engaged to someone else."

Rob listened intently.

"So, he followed her. Watched her while she went about her daily life, maybe even through her bedroom window, or with her new man. You get the picture."

Rob nodded again.

"He would have fantasised about her, about harming her or

forcing her to have sexual intercourse with him, but he didn't have the courage to act on it."

"I can see where this is going," croaked Rob.

"As his obsession increased, so did his fantasies until one day he threatened her."

"Would he have killed her?"

"Probably not at that stage, but as he got bolder, he may have used more force, until one day he did it. Once he realised the satisfaction he got from it, he would have wanted to do it again."

"Christ," said Rob. "So, this guy will have a history of this sort of thing?"

"Indeed. He probably also moved around a lot to stay off the radar. A trail of dead bodies has a way of grabbing attention."

"So, looking at cold cases in Surrey would be a waste of time?" Rob made a mental note to tell Jenny to widen the search area.

"Maybe not, but you'd have more luck looking nationwide."

Rob exhaled slowly through his mouth. This was huge. His personal vendetta case had snowballed into a nationwide serial killer hunt, the press was going to go ape-shit. "How many times do you think this guy's done this?"

Tony shrugged. "It's hard to say. Less sophisticated offenders usually find their victims through opportunity. There's not much in the way of planning. The crime scenes are messy, unthought-through."

"This guy's not like that," said Rob.

"I know." Tony gave him a hard stare. "Your guy has been planning this for a while. He mapped out her route home, he knew her routine inside out. He's showing a remarkable level of sophistication and intelligence in his planning, which means he's fairly advanced."

"Not a beginner, then?" Rob attempted to lighten the mood, but it fell flat.

"No. I'd say your guy has been doing this for some time."

. . .

ROB CALLED DCI Lawrence the moment he left the pub.

"Have you got something?" barked the DCI down the phone without even saying hello.

"Possibly. Can I come and see you?"

Sam Lawrence lived in a big house on Richmond Hill with his wife, Diana, and their two girls. The girls went to a local prep school and Diana, who was an interior designer, worked mornings so she had the afternoons free to devote to the school run, homework and making tea. Rob had met Lawrence's wife before and liked her, although their meeting had been brief. Lawrence wasn't a big fan of mixing business with his family life, which is probably why his marriage had survived when so many others had failed.

He remembered his boss mentioning how he liked to leave his work at the door when he went home, that way the ugliness didn't seep into the other areas of his life. It was great in theory, but Rob wondered how often he actually managed to do that. It was hard, if not impossible to switch off some days, today being a classic case in point.

A pause. "Sure. Come now."

Rob parked outside the three-storey Victorian terrace on leafy Mount Ararat Drive. Lawrence had put up a new fence since the last time he was there. This one was an imposing six foot and made of thick wrought-iron. It had diamond-shaped daggers on the tips of the vertical poles and made the house hiding beyond seem colder and more unwelcoming.

He rang the buzzer and immediately the gate swung open. Lawrence opened the front door before Rob made it to the top step.

"Come on in." He stood back to let Rob enter. The DCI was wearing a tracksuit, which was so out of character that Rob did a double-take as he walked through the door.

"I've been exercising," Lawrence said, by way of explanation.

The interior was stylishly done, thanks to Diane's excellent taste and business acumen. Rob had heard a rumour that the couple had inherited the house from Diane's parents. Certainly, it was way beyond the scope of a DCI's salary. The floorboards were a pale wood and wider than usual, creating a sense of space. Unlike most Victorian houses, you really felt you could breathe in this one. There was a rustic eight-seater wooden table at the one end of the open-plan living-dining room, while a right-angled leather sofa and matching armchair were positioned at the other. On the wall, a massive flat-screen television showed a football game with the sound on mute.

Lawrence gestured to the wooden table. He didn't want Rob making himself too comfy. This wasn't going to be a long visit.

Rob wondered where Diana and the girls were. Probably upstairs, asked to stay out of the way, to prevent the ugliness from seeping.

Rob sat down and declined a beer. The last one was still sitting in his gullet making him feel sick. The acrid taste in his mouth was a constant reminder of why he'd come.

"What have you got for me?" Lawrence got straight to the point.

Rob took a deep breath and said, "You're not going to like this."

Lawrence gave him a thousand-yard stare.

"It seems we've got a serial rapist and murderer on the loose."

Lawrence was quiet for a full minute and Rob could almost hear the cogs grinding in his head. Eventually he said, "It was the ring, wasn't it?"

"Yeah."

Lawrence banged his fist down on the table. "I knew something like this was going to happen. It never fucking rains but it pours."

Rob waited for the rant to end.

"Now we'll have the Yard banging down our door demanding a piece of this, and we'll have to open the case up to other departments because we don't have the resources to hunt a serial killer." His piercing eyes fixed on Rob. "Are you sure about this?"

Rob nodded. "I spoke to my friend Tony Sanderson this evening. He's the…"

"I know who he is," interjected Lawrence. "Works for the secret bloody service as a profiler, mostly counter-terrorism stuff. Didn't he write that book, *Mind Games,* about this very thing?"

"Yeah." Tony was something of a national superstar. Most of the crime agencies had consulted with him at some point or other.

"And you told him about our case?" He gave Rob a hard look, daring him to deny it.

Rob didn't bother. "Yup. It was the ring that convinced him. It's ritualistic, it has relevance. Tony reckons the guy was jilted as a youngster, which makes sense given his obvious anger towards women."

"Lots of people are jilted," muttered Lawrence. "That doesn't make them all serial killers." He had a point. "But I get what he's saying," he continued wearily. "We're going to have to open up the search if we want to catch this guy. I take it Sanderson thinks he's done this before?"

"Yeah, and he said he probably moved around a lot too, to avoid detection, so we'll have to look at all county records."

Lawrence nodded slowly. "Okay, but I'm not going to the press with this until we have a lead on this guy. If looking at cold cases helps us catch him, that's fantastic, but we still only have one dead body, so there's no need to create mayhem."

Yet, thought Rob, but he didn't say so.

If Tony was right, it was only a matter of time before the stalker struck again.

7

Rob got home to find Yvette standing in the hall wearing nothing but black lace underwear and a suspender belt. Soft, satin straps crisscrossed her lithe, tanned body connecting all the parts to each other. The expression on her face did not say *come to bed*, however, but rather *what the hell time do you call this?*

"I'm sorry," he began, his eyes roaming over her outfit. He felt the familiar stirring he always felt when he was with her. "Have you been waiting long?"

"Only about three hours," she said in a huff. "You said you'd be back by nine."

He had. He'd texted her on the way to the pub before he'd met Tony, but in all fairness, he hadn't expected the conversation to turn out the way it had. In light of what had happened, he'd forgotten all about his promise to Yvette.

"Something came up," he said, realising how clichéd that sounded.

"Something always does." She gave him a sad look. "But it isn't going to be you. I'm cold and tired, and I'm going to bed. I just wanted you to see what you missed."

Rob closed the distance between them. "You're not going to tease me like this then disappear," he said, reaching for her. "I was looking forward to unravelling you."

She stiffened. He could tell she was beyond the point of relenting. He'd pushed it too far this time.

"I'm not in the mood anymore." She turned and padded barefoot up the stairs. "Don't forget to turn the heating off before you come to bed. I've had it on high while I've been waiting."

She certainly knew how to make him feel guilty.

With a heavy sigh, he walked into the lounge, sat down and took off his shoes. God, he was tired. It was just as well Yvette wasn't in the mood anymore, because quite frankly, he wasn't sure he could muster the energy tonight. Tony's revelation had shocked him more than he cared to admit, but the more he thought about it, the more obvious it seemed. Why hadn't he seen it sooner? He'd read Tony's book, he should have considered all the options.

He leaned his head back onto the headrest and closed his eyes. Ironically, it was the ring that had made him think it was personal. Like the murderer quite literally saying, *this is what you can do with your engagement ring.*

He was just drifting off to sleep when a thought struck him. If Julie wasn't the first, and she wasn't someone he knew, then how had the stalker targeted her? How had he known she was engaged? He took out his phone, noticing with a grimace that the battery was nearly dead, but not wanting to interrupt his train of thought, he didn't get up to plug it in. Instead, he made a list.

Newspaper announcement?

Wedding cake?

Dress?

Wedding planner?

He'd found her somehow, and it was most likely something to

do with the wedding. He made a mental note to call Justin King the next day and ask him about their wedding plans. Then weariness overcame him, and he fell asleep, without plugging in his phone.

"Cold cases," he told his team at the squad meeting the next morning. "Anything with the same MO. It doesn't matter where it is. This guy could have moved around."

"Shall we stay on the CCTV?" Simon, one of the dozen officers assigned to the video studio wanted to know.

"Please. I still think that's how we're going to ID this guy. We've got to catch him on camera. He followed her around for weeks. There must be a clear shot of him somewhere."

He'd outlined the serial killer theory to the wide-eyed excitement of the team, all of whom were still fairly young, but he did remind them there was still only one victim, so while the theory made sense, they were focused on finding Julie's killer first and foremost.

"Let's not get distracted by this," he'd instructed them. "Our priority is Julie Andrews."

The public appeal had resulted in hundreds of new leads, which the Twickenham branch were sifting through before passing on. His inbox was overflowing and there were several messages to call DCI Douglas back at Twickenham Police Station.

"I've got a caller who saw a man matching your description at Costa Coffee at Kew Retail Park around five o'clock on Friday afternoon. The timing fits, yes?" DCI Douglas sounded like an efficient, capable detective.

A little shot of adrenalin surged through his veins. "Yes, and the location. The retail park is around the corner from the National Archives."

DCI Douglas passed on the woman's number, and once Rob

had thanked him and hung up, he dialled her. She sounded breathy, like she'd been running, and there was a low drone in the background.

"Hello, Mrs. Hawes?"

"Yes?"

"This is Detective Inspector Rob Miller from the Richmond Police Station. I believe you phoned our request line earlier today?"

"Oh, yes. I did. Hang on, let me turn the Hoover off."

The drone stopped.

"Could you tell me about the man you saw?" he asked when she came back on the line, trying not to sound overly eager.

"Well, I noticed him because he was sitting at the table next to me outside Costa in a tracksuit top with the hood up. He asked me for a light. When I saw the appeal on the news, I thought, that sounds just like the guy I saw. So, I called it in."

A smoker?

"Did you get a good look at him? Could you describe him to me?"

"Yeah, I suppose so. His hood was up, but then it was cold outside. He had a thin face; quite angular features and he was wearing spectacles."

"Spectacles, are you sure?"

"Yes, he was reading the newspaper. "

"And smoking?"

"Yes."

Two more things to add to their description of him, *if* this was the right guy.

"Anything else you can remember about him? Did he have any tattoos or earrings, for example?"

"No, nothing like that. He looked quite clean and well-dressed actually, apart from the hoodie. He was very tall, his legs jutted out under the table."

"Did he seem stressed to you? Was he fidgeting, agitated?"

"No, nothing like that. In fact, just the opposite. He seemed fairly relaxed."

He pressed her for a bit longer, but she couldn't remember anything else. Eventually, he thanked her and let her go.

He wanted to believe this was their guy, really wanted to, but something inside of him told him to proceed with caution. The last thing they needed was to go chasing after a red herring. Would the stalker – a man about to execute a carefully thought-out attack – be sitting at a coffee shop smoking a cigarette and reading the newspaper like he didn't have a care in the world?

It didn't seem likely. Still, they couldn't ignore the information. The location was spot-on, the archives being less than two-hundred metres from the retail park. He could have been waiting for her to finish work. He'd know she came out at six, he knew her routine.

He got up and went to the CCTV suite.

"I've just had a call from a woman who thinks she saw the stalker at Costa Coffee in Kew Retail Park on Friday afternoon around five p.m. Can someone get onto them for any security cameras they've got in the area? The retail park must have several."

Celeste nodded. "I'll get right on it, sir."

He forced a smile. The CCTV crew had been working in eight-hour shifts, around the clock and they were bleary-eyed and pasty like they needed a good dose of sunlight. "This is good news. If he was there, we'll get him."

Back at his desk, he tried calling the management company again. It rang several times and he was just about to hang up when a young woman answered the phone.

Finally.

He introduced himself and told her what he was after.

She said she'd get her manager to call him back. She

confirmed there were two cameras on the premises, but she didn't know where or how to get the video feed to him. He gave her his direct line and stressed the urgency. Ten minutes later, a Mr. Patel called him back. He was very sorry, but as it's a new block they hadn't got around to installing the security software yet, so even though they had the cameras installed, they weren't operational.

Rob slammed the phone down. "What bloody good is a security camera if it's not operational?" he ranted to Mallory who'd just walked into his office and was now considering exiting and coming back later. Mallory was in charge of following up the cold cases.

"We've got a possible related case." He hovered by the door.

Rob beckoned him in. "Tell me."

Mallory took a seat opposite him. "Two years ago, in South Yorkshire, the body of a young woman was found out on the moors. The post-mortem confirmed she'd been raped and strangled."

Rob sat up straight. "Sounds like it could be our man. Who was the investigating officer?"

"A DCI Moorcroft, South Yorkshire Police. No one was ever charged. Here's the file." He put a hardcopy down on Rob's desk.

"Have you spoken to him?"

"Yes, he's at a symposium in Manchester this week, but he'll be back at his desk on Friday."

"Bugger that," said Rob getting up. He was itching to do something. "We don't have till Friday, by then the case will have been handed over to the Yard's murder squad. Manchester's not that far away. Where's the symposium?"

"I didn't ask."

"Find out." Rob was already pulling on his jacket. "You and I are heading up there now. I'll drive."

The journey to Manchester took just under four and a half hours. It would have been less except they got caught up in some bad traffic around Birmingham. The Radisson Hotel, where the police symposium on knife crime was being held was out by the airport, which thankfully meant they didn't have to navigate the city centre.

They parked in the vast carpark and made their way inside. The lobby was a hive of uniformed policemen and plain-clothed officers walking in and out. The café next door, and connected to the hotel, was also packed. They followed signs to the conference facility on the first floor only to discover the symposium had adjourned for tea.

"Do you know where I might find DCI Moorcroft?" Rob asked a suited, middle-aged man standing in the doorway.

"He's Sheffield Police, isn't he?" The man's brow furrowed. "You'll probably find him in the café downstairs. That's where most of them have gone."

Rob thanked him, and they went back downstairs.

"How the hell are we going to find this guy?" Mallory gazed at the sea of police officers milling around, holding take-away cups of coffee.

"You got his mobile number?" asked Rob.

Mallory grinned and pulled out his phone. He made the call and they waited to see who'd reach for their phone. A short, stocky man with dark hair and even darker eyebrows reached into his pocket. He pulled out his phone and stared at the screen. Before he had time to answer it, Rob walked up to him. "Are you DCI Moorcroft?"

At the man's suspicious nod, he said, "I'm DCI Rob Miller from Richmond CID and this is DS Mallory. May we have a word, please?"

Moorcroft frowned causing his eyebrows to meet in the middle. He pocketed his phone. "What's this about?" He had a strong Yorkshire accent and beady eyes that seemed to stare right through you.

Mallory said, "I left a message on your phone earlier today. It's in connection with the young lady you found on the moors two years ago."

"Greta Ansley?" The words came quickly to his lips, like a memory never forgotten.

Rob, who hadn't had time to read the file and didn't know the girl's name, glanced at Mallory. His deputy nodded. "That's the one."

"Let's talk in here." Moorcroft guided them into the lobby which was less packed than the café. There were no free seats, so they stood to the left of the entrance, out of the main thorough-fare. "What is it you want to know?"

"You didn't charge anyone with the murder?" Rob asked.

Moorcroft sighed. "No, we looked at the boyfriend, or rather fiancé, but he had a watertight alibi for the night of the murder."

Mallory glanced at Rob, who felt his pulse quicken. "Fiancé? So, she was engaged when she was killed?" He did his best to keep his voice steady.

"Yes, it was tragic. Her fiancé was devastated. They were due to marry the following weekend." Rob sensed his frustration. It was clear Moorcroft had never got over it.

"Was there anything else significant about the crime?" asked Rob. "How did you find her? Were her hands bound?"

A light went on behind Moorcroft's eyes. "Her hands weren't bound, no, but she had deep bruises on her forearms which implied he'd been kneeling on them to pin her down. She'd been knocked around a bit, probably lost consciousness before she was raped." He grimaced. "We can hope anyway. It looked like she'd tried to fight off her attacker."

"Any DNA?" asked Rob knowing the answer but asking anyway. If there was, it would have been mentioned in the report.

Moorcroft shook his head. "Unfortunately, no. Not under her

nails or inside her. He must have used protection. Why do you ask?"

Rob exhaled slowly. "We have a young lady who was killed in a similar manner to your victim."

A pause. Then Moorcroft said, "How similar?"

"Enough to warrant further investigation," said Rob.

"You think they're related?"

"I think it's possible," Rob said carefully. "Was there anything else significant about the way you found her?"

Moorcroft gave him a hard look. "You can read the pathologist's report if it'll make you feel better."

Mallory said, "Was she wearing her engagement ring?"

The DCI shook his head. "No, she wasn't. We couldn't find it on her and her fiancé said it wasn't at home, so we assumed the bastard had stolen it."

"It wasn't anywhere on the body?" pressed Rob.

"I'm positive. We never found it."

"Could you get the post-mortem report for us?" asked Mallory. "We'd like to have a look at it."

Moorcroft reached for his phone. "Sure, I'll fire off an email now. Where did you say you were based again?"

"Richmond, Surrey." Rob gave him a card with his contact details on. "Thanks very much."

"NOT QUITE THE SAME MO, THEN?" Mallory said as they walked back to the car, leaving the hubbub of the police symposium behind them.

Rob shrugged. "It's hard to tell. This was two years ago, don't forget. He could still have been perfecting his MO, so to speak."

Tony's words echoed in his mind.

Less sophisticated offenders usually find their victims through opportunity. There's not much in the way of planning. The crime scenes are messy, unthought-through.

"Perhaps, he was just starting out when he attacked this girl." Rob thought out loud. "His technique wasn't as polished. He took the ring as a memento but didn't think to insert it into his victim. He hadn't got to that level yet."

Mallory stared at him. "She could have been his first."

"Or his last before Julie," said Rob, but he knew as soon as he said it that it was unlikely. The degree of planning in Julie's murder implied the stalker had spent a long time perfecting his technique. Rob was willing to bet there were others between them. They just hadn't linked them yet.

"We have to consider that it may not be the same bloke at all." Mallory pointed out once they reached the car. "Do you want me to drive back?"

Rob chucked him the car keys. He wanted to use the time to think. "Thanks."

They got in and Mallory started the engine. Rob turned to him. "This girl, Greta, was also engaged. That's a massive coincidence, don't you think? I hear what you're saying, but I'm tending towards believing it's the same bloke."

Mallory pulled out of the carpark. "Yeah. Too massive."

8

Tonight, was the night.

It was dark. The moon, or what was left of it, was a silver sliver in the night sky. Tomorrow or the day after it would be a new moon, but the stalker didn't want to wait that long.

He was ready.

The familiar sense of anticipation built inside him, causing butterflies in his stomach. Tonight, Sara would pay for Bridget's betrayal, just like Julie had, just like Greta and the others had. He would never stop making *her* pay.

His Bridget.

She'd been so young and innocent when he'd first met her. He still remembered her wide, toothy grin and how her eyes had lit up as she'd smiled at him across the lecture hall. He used to think there was magic in her gaze, the way it warmed him up inside. No one else had been able to warm him the way Bridget had.

He forced his attention back to Sara, jogging up the street. He watched her ponytail swish to and fro like a horse's tail, her legs moving in an easy rhythm. She was coming towards him up the road, the light on her forehead not yet on. Tonight, for some reason, she wasn't wearing her visibility jacket. He took that as a sign. The universe was telling him tonight was the night. In a few minutes, she'd run right past him and swing left into the park.

He turned his back as she passed, but he was in the shadow of an ancient oak tree, so she wouldn't have noticed him. No one noticed him.

Except Bridget.

Once in the park, she switched on her head lamp and ran down Sawyer's Hill towards Sheen Gate, keeping to the dirt track which ran parallel to the road. Even though the inner park street was devoid of cars, it was filled with cyclists taking advantage of the clear roads, which made the gravel track the safer option. Another sign.

He knew her route by heart. It would take her twenty minutes to reach Sheen Gate, after which she'd turn around and run back along the gravel path past East Sheen Common and Bishop's Pond. It was the darkest section of her run, flanked by wooded areas and tall, bushy bracken, and the place where he would be waiting.

He strolled along the footpath as if going for an evening walk until he reached a densely wooded area behind which was an eight-foot brick wall.

No escape.

He felt in his jacket pocket for the duct-tape, the end already neatly folded back so he could rip it off at a moment's notice. He couldn't afford to waste time. Not that anyone was around.

He checked his watch. Not long now.

He stood silently behind a thick tree trunk, listening to the myriad of little insects as they scurried about searching for food. The ground was littered with acorns which crunched when he trod on them, but he wasn't too worried because she wore earphones which would drown out any sound he might make.

Then, he heard her footsteps, light and regular, approaching from along the path. He pulled up his balaclava and peered out from behind the tree, invisible in the darkness. The bright light of her headgear hovered above her like some alien contraption. Her breathing was laboured, he heard it clearly as she got closer. She liked to push herself along this bit, the final leg of her run. Five metres away... four... three... two. Then he stepped out and with a quick swipe of his arm, he hit her in the neck. She went down hard, her feet sliding out underneath her. She landed on the gravel, gasping, her chest heaving from her run and from the shock of the surprise attack.

How easy was that?

He dragged her by the ponytail into the trees, not bothered by the strangled crying sound she was making. With her larynx damaged by his blow, it wasn't loud enough for anyone to hear.

Not that anyone was around.

He reached for the tape and in a practised move, whipped it several times around her wrists to prevent her from scratching him. One had to be so careful these days. Then, he sat on top of her while she bucked and twisted beneath him. Her skin was moist with perspiration, her eyes wild with fear.

God, how he loved this part.

She opened her mouth to scream but he was ready for her. He stuck a section of tape over her mouth to muffle the sound.

"Hush," he told her in a soft voice. "It'll all be over soon."

IT WAS early morning and the sun was still hovering on the horizon when Rob got to the crime scene. He knew Richmond Park from his younger days when he used to come here for picnics with his mates. They'd sit on a blanket and drink cheap wine and talk and laugh, maybe play a bit of footie. It still looked the same, although for him, everything had changed. Those carefree days were long gone, and as he gazed into the low-lying mist that hung above the bracken, yet to be burned off by the sun, he felt a sudden longing for those innocent days when the world still made sense.

"Over here, guv," called Mallory, who looked like he hadn't slept a wink. After they'd got back from their trip up north, they'd returned to the station where they'd been occupied following up the various lines of enquiry. Rob had called it a day around ten pm, conscious of Yvette waiting for him at home, but Mallory had still been there when he'd left.

He needn't have bothered, Yvette was still giving him the silent treatment. He wasn't sure he even knew why. So, he'd slept on the couch and despite his mind working overtime, he managed to get a solid six hours. That was good going for the middle of an investigation.

He walked along the gravel path, past a pretty pond with a giant heron standing on one leg in the shallows. A herd of unsuspecting deer grazed in the distance, oblivious to the events of the night before. After a while, the path grew cooler and darker as it wound through a wooded area. Oaks, elms and plane trees fought for space amongst the knee-high shrubs and bushes. Underfoot and hidden beneath the long grass was a tangled mesh of brambles and nettles. He carefully stepped over them to get to the forensic tent that had been set up to protect the victim's body. Like before, it was illuminated within, giving it an eerie glow.

"What have we got?" he asked Mallory, pausing to pull on the coveralls handed to him by a police officer guarding the scene. Mallory was already kitted up.

"Another young woman." The shadows beneath his eyes were almost purple. "A jogger. She's got no ID on her, but by the looks of things, it's the same guy."

Rob nodded and lifted the flap. A pathologist was bending over a slim, dark-haired woman in her mid-twenties dressed in running gear. She'd been strangled by a thick elastic cord attached to a mechanism of some kind."

"What is that around her neck?" he asked Mallory.

"It's a headlamp, cyclists and joggers often wear them at night."

They went inside, the flap dropping behind them, cutting off any semblance of normality. The crime scene was all that mattered now. Without speaking, Rob absorbed the image in front of him. The victim's hands were bound, like Julie's, in the same way, above her head and secured to a tree trunk with tape. Her leggings and underwear had been ripped down to below her knees and one trainer had come off, possibly in the struggle. He didn't need to ask if she'd been sexually assaulted, he could see the bruising and dried blood on her inner thighs.

"Jesus," he muttered, averting his eyes. He moved around to get a better look at her face. "She's so young."

"This one wasn't punched in the face," said Mallory, stating the obvious. Her skin was clear and smooth, and she had high cheekbones and full, sensual lips. She would have been extremely attractive without the pasty hue of death that clung to her like a plastic film.

"He managed to subdue her without much force." Rob studied her wrists. "There is some bruising, but she didn't struggle as much as Julie."

"Any chance of getting some DNA off that tape?" he asked the pathologist, who was carefully peeling it off her wrists and inserting it into a clear, plastic evidence bag. His smooth movements belied the tension visible in his clenched jaw.

"It's possible." He glanced up. "Especially if he tore it off with his teeth."

"Okay, good." Might as well hope for the best. You never knew what might transpire. Cases had been solved on less. Eventually, this guy had to slip up and leave a trace. Every new victim meant more contact and more chance of a transfer of DNA.

"What about the ring?" whispered Mallory. A crime scene photographer was taking pictures, working in synergy with the pathologist. Every piece of evidence that was bagged, was first photographed in situ on the victim.

Rob lowered his voice and asked the pathologist to check inside the victim for a ring. The man's eyes widened, but he did as he was told.

"At first glance, I can't see anything, but that's not to say it's not there. I'll be able look more thoroughly when I get her back to the lab. There's only so much I can do out here."

Fair enough. He'd have to wait. "Okay, thanks."

Rob let his eyes linger over her broken and defiled body one last time, then left the tent, giving in to a sudden need for fresh air. "Has anyone reported her missing?"

"I've been on to uniform who are going to get back to us in the next half hour. She had nothing on her, no purse or ID of any kind."

"She must be local," remarked Rob. "If she had a partner or a parent, they'll have reported her missing when she didn't return from her run."

On cue, Mallory's mobile rang. He held up a finger and listened intently. When he hung up, he said, "It's possible she's a local woman called Sara Bakshi. And get this, her fiancé reported her missing last night around eleven o'clock."

Sara's fiancé lived in an impressive Victorian townhouse that stretched up four storeys on the upper section of Queen's Road, Richmond, next to the American University campus. At one point, the houses along Queen's Road were probably owned by wealthy noblemen – indeed the Royal hunting lodge was situated just inside Richmond Park – but most of the properties were now subdivided and the leasehold shared by different landlords.

Rob counted five buzzers on the wall next to the massive front door. There was a basement flat in addition to the ground floor and the three above. This door, however, seemed to cater for the ground floor apartment only. The basement entrance was at the side of the building and access to the upper floors was at the back of the house. An equally impressive Porsche SUV stood in the driveway, along with a fashionable Mini Cooper in racing green. On the other side of the gravel carpark stood a gleaming, silver Mercedes convertible.

"People around here aren't short of a few bob," remarked Mallory, as he pressed the ground floor buzzer next to the name Gareth Conrad.

A man whose height was inversely proportional to the size of his SUV opened the door. He was in socks, which made him appear even shorter. From where he stood, Rob looked down onto the guy's bald patch.

The man craned his neck to look up at them. "I'm Gareth, Sara's fiancé, please come inside."

They followed him into a spacious lounge with cream carpeting and leather furniture. The curtains were soft and silky, and held open with gold rope so the struggling sunlight could enter. A glass coffee table stood in the centre of the room containing a huge bunch of white lilies. Directly above the lilies was a modern light fixture that looked as if it had been constructed from a myriad of little paper hexagons, which somehow managed to fit together in a sort of ill-fitting puzzle. The overall effect was bright and stylish.

Rob took a seat on the armchair leaving Mallory to sit beside Gareth on the couch.

"I take it you have news of Sara?" Gareth asked in a voice used to giving commands. Rob had been told he worked for Price Waterhouse Coopers in London's financial district. He studied the man's face. There was worry behind the eyes, but he was trying hard not to show it. Perhaps he'd been taught showing emotion was weakness. Keep bluffing till you can't anymore. He was an investment banker, after all.

"Yes, we do. I'm sorry to have to tell you this, Mr. Conrad, but we found a body in Richmond Park this morning which we believe to be Sara."

"A body?" He stared at them without blinking for a long moment as he tried to process what he'd just heard.

Rob gave him a moment.

"We'd like you to identify her, if at all possible? But, when you're ready."

Gareth nodded blankly. His voice was croaky when he asked, "How did she die?"

"She was attacked." He hesitated. "It looks like she was strangled."

Gareth gave a shuddering gasp, then dropped his head into his hands. Mallory met Rob's eye, but Rob gave a miniscule shake of his head. Gareth didn't need to know the rest. Not yet.

"Do you feel up to answering a few questions?" Rob asked, after a moment.

The banker nodded and slowly removed his hands from his face leaving a blotchy imprint. "I don't understand how this happened? I got home last night and she wasn't here. At first, I assumed she'd gone for her run, as usual, but when she didn't come home, I thought maybe she'd met a friend for a drink or something."

"Did you try calling her?" asked Mallory.

"Yes, repeatedly. She didn't pick up. That's when I got worried. She wouldn't go out all night without telling me."

"Is that when you called the police?" again Mallory, who was making notes in his book.

"I called 999 at about eleven and reported her missing. I was frantic, by then. I thought about going to look for her, but it didn't seem realistic since I had no idea where she'd gone. Perhaps, if I'd walked through the park..."

"It would have been too late," Rob said gently. "There's nothing you could have done."

Gareth sat quietly as the reality sunk in.

"Do you know who did this?" he eventually asked.

Rob wanted to give him some hope, but they were so far from catching the guy, it was embarrassing. He couldn't very well say they hadn't the foggiest. He settled for a compromise. "We think it's the same man who attacked a young woman in Kew last week."

"We're following several lines of enquiry," added Mallory. "It won't be long before we have something."

Rob was impressed by his colleague's show of confidence. He only wished he felt the same. So far, the perpetrator had avoided leaving any DNA, any images on CCTV, and indeed any trace of himself at the crime scenes. He thought of Sara's body and the duct-tape over her mouth. Maybe this time...

"When did you get engaged?" asked Mallory, getting into the line of questioning they'd discussed on the way there.

Gareth didn't need to think about it. "Valentine's Day. I'd been planning it for some time."

A month and a half ago. "And how did you two meet?"

"Oh, we met in the Greek Islands. Mykonos, actually. She was on holiday with some girlfriends and I was sailing around the Cyclades with work colleagues. We met at a beach bar and hit it off straight away. It was love at first sight, you might say."

"That's very romantic," said Mallory wistfully, earning himself a raised eyebrow from Rob. He cleared his throat. "And so how long were you dating before you proposed?"

"Eight months. We met in June last year."

That was when he'd met Yvette, thought Rob. It was long enough to know you loved someone.

Mallory pushed on. "Was Sara wearing an engagement ring?

Rob had waited six months before he'd proposed on
Christmas Eve. It had been just the two of them, and they'd spent
a long, boozy day in bed drinking champagne and making love.
He hadn't known why this beautiful, sexy woman had chosen him,
but he'd thought he'd better propose before she changed her
mind. Luckily, she'd said yes.

Conrad was nodding. "Yes, she wore a four-carat solitaire in a
white gold band. Why do you ask? Is it missing?"

There were no flies on this guy.

"We didn't find it on her body," Rob told him. They'd know
more after the post-mortem.

"I'll have to let the insurance company know." Conrad stopped
and looked a little shocked that he'd said that. "Sorry, this is so
surreal. It's still sinking in."

"That's okay, we understand." Rob took a deep breath, then
said, "Can I ask what might seem like a strange question? Did Sara
mention anyone following her or watching her over the last few
days? Or weeks?" he added as an afterthought. Justin King, Julie's
fiancé, had said the stalker had backed off in the last week, so
perhaps he'd found his new target by then?

Sara.

The stalker had known Julie's routine, so all he had to do was
wait for the right moment. But while he was waiting, he'd moved
on to the next woman. Could it be he was escalating his activity?
Needing more and more in order to satisfy himself?

*Once he realised the satisfaction he got from it, he would have
wanted to do it again.*

9

"Actually, Sara did think someone was following her, but that was over a week ago. I thought she was being paranoid."

"Was she prone to paranoia?" asked Rob.

"No, not at all." He rubbed a hand over his bald spot, pressing the fly-away hair back into place. "That's not what I meant. I thought she'd been mistaken, that's all. This guy followed her from the King's Road in Sloane Square to Knightsbridge last Saturday, then she saw him again outside the house when she got home. That was the weird part, the bit that made her suspect he was following her. But she could have been mistaken, right? It could have been a different guy?"

Or the same guy.

"Did she mention what he looked like?" asked Mallory.

"Only that he was tall, thin and wore a dark hoodie."

Mallory met Rob's gaze, then turned back to Conrad. "Did she get a look at his face?"

"All she said was he was thin and had facial hair."

"Facial hair? Like a beard?" asked Mallory.

Gareth nodded.

"Okay." Rob sighed. It was the same old story. No way to identify the guy. "What time was she in King's Road last Saturday?" He turned to Mallory. "Let's see if we can get the CCTV from that area."

Mallory nodded and took out his phone.

Gareth frowned. "I'm not sure. It could have been around midday. I think she met a friend for lunch, then did a bit of shopping. She got home just after five. That's all I know."

"That's a start." Rob offered a wry smile. "Were you here when she got back?"

"Yeah. I was watching the football." A pause. Then he said, "Is the stalker the same guy who killed that other girl? The one in Kew?"

"We think so, yes."

There was a pause, then he scanned Rob's face. "The papers said she was raped."

Rob gave him a frank stare. There was no point in candy-coating it. Gareth's shoulders slunk forward and the resilience that had been holding him up until now ebbed away. His voice wobbled as he asked, "But why Sara? Why would he target her?"

And that, Rob acknowledged to himself, was the million-dollar question.

"I don't know," he said honestly. "But we plan to find out. There must be something linking the girls together."

He organised his thoughts, giving Conrad a moment to compose himself. "Did Sara work? Did she have a particular routine? Anything that might help shed some light on her movements in the last week?"

Conrad thought for a moment. "She was preoccupied with planning the wedding. So, she was meeting with the wedding planner, going for dress fittings, that sort of thing."

"Presumably, Julie would have been doing the same," Mallory

said under his breath.

"Do you have the wedding planner's details?" asked Rob. "Do you know where she bought the dress?"

"I don't know much about the dress, that was a secret, but her mother might know, or her best friend, Vivian. I can give you their numbers. I think I have an email on my laptop from the wedding planner, but then so will Sara. She'll have it all on hers. Shall I get it for you?"

"That would be a great help," said Rob. Hopefully, all her wedding contacts would be on her laptop, so they could run a check against Julie's contacts. It might give them an idea as to how the stalker was targeting his victims.

"Is there anything else you can think of," asked Rob when Gareth returned holding Sara's laptop like it was a tray laden with fine china. He took it from him. "What we need is her movements over the last week, so we can locate this guy on CCTV."

Gareth pressed his lips together. "Hmm... I'm not sure what her daily routine was because I'm not here in the day. I work in the city and get back around seven. I know she often goes for a jog in the evening, but as to her movements during the day, I'm afraid I can't help you much with that."

"She doesn't work then?"

"No, not anymore. She used to be an account's assistant and did temporary work but her last contract ended a month ago."

Obviously, her fiancé was okay with her not working.

As if reading his thoughts, Conrad added, "We were planning to start a family as soon as possible. Sara's always wanted a big family being an only child and I'm not getting any younger."

Rob studied the short, balding man. Despite the premature hair loss, he must be mid to late thirties. Still plenty of time. Rob wondered if he ought to be more concerned about things like that. Yvette had made her feelings quite clear on the subject – no kids – so he'd put it out of his mind, but a big family did sound nice.

Lots of little rug-rats running around. He wondered briefly if he was making a mistake. They hadn't even settled on a date yet. It seemed enough just to be engaged. There was no urgency, certainly not on his side, and he didn't think on hers either. Perhaps it was time they had a talk.

They questioned Conrad until it was clear he had nothing more to add, then they returned to Richmond Police Station.

"Can I have your attention, please?" Rob stood in front of his team in Incident Room 2. About two dozen weary but hopeful faces stared back at him. The late nights and relentless sifting through CCTV footage were beginning to tell. They now had two dead bodies instead of one and double the pressure. They needed a lead soon. So far, all their efforts had turned up zilch.

"As you know, a second victim, Sara Bakshi, was found in Richmond Park this morning. Same MO as our other victim, Julie Andrews. We're pretty confident this is the same guy." He paused and looked at Mallory who was pinning a photograph they'd got from Sara's fiancé to the whiteboard beside the one taken at the crime scene. It had been taken on a trip to Paris, the Eiffel Tower clearly visible in the background. The sky was a perfect blue and Sara smiled into the camera like she didn't have a care in the world. "She was also engaged. Now that is a hell of a coincidence, so we suspect the wedding angle is how he's finding his victims."

There were a few nods and murmurs. They knew what was coming.

"For those of you not on CCTV duty, please can you look into Julie and Sara's wedding arrangements? We need to find similarities between them like whether they both used the same wedding planner, dressmaker or booked the same venue – all that stuff. Look for links between the girls, anything that will help us connect them together. Got it?"

Nods all round.

Rob continued, "I've got some more information on Sara's

movements this last week. It turns out she told her fiancé that she thought someone was following her, and you guessed it, he was tall and wearing a hoodie. According to her fiancé, she never got a good look at his face."

Murmurs of frustration.

"He may also be growing some facial hair. Now, I know this guy's good at keeping himself hidden, but don't give up, we'll get him eventually. It's just a matter of time. Some camera somewhere will pick him up. It has to. We just have to find it."

Rob handed over to Mallory. "Sara Bakshi had lunch with a friend in Kings Road near Sloane Square last Saturday. I'm afraid we don't know where. It was the day after Julie was murdered, so our killer didn't waste any time selecting his next victim."

"CCTV team, you know what you have to do," said Rob, breaking the horrified silence that had ensued after Mallory's statement. "Anything along the King's Road on Saturday from eleven onwards. Apparently, she walked to Knightsbridge, then took the tube back to Richmond, where she spotted him again outside her apartment. Her address is on the board. Also, if you can ping her phone location, it might backup her route, provided, of course, that she had it switched on. Luke, will you look into that?"

"I'll get right on it."

"Thanks. Okay, that's it for now."

They filed out in silence. Rob wasn't sure if it was sheer tiredness or waning enthusiasm. He hoped the former, but it was probably both. They weren't getting any closer to the killer, and the bodies were piling up. The killer was escalating, getting greedy. Two bodies in two weeks. As much as it pained him to admit it, he very much feared it wouldn't be long before they had another one on their hands.

He turned to Mallory. "We've got to stop this guy. Somehow, there's a link between these two girls. We've got to find it."

Mallory nodded sagely. He too could sense the team morale sagging.

"I know."

THE POST-MORTEM WAS CONDUCTED that afternoon at precisely three o'clock, but it was gone half-past by the time Rob got there. It was the same guy as before. Gowan.

"Sorry, I'm late," called Rob from the viewing gallery. He wasn't going down for this one, there wasn't time. The body of Sara Bakshi lay on the metal table, sliced open from sternum to stomach, her insides on display. Rob focused on the doctor's face, rather than the corpse. "What have I missed?"

"I started with an internal inspection, considering she was raped," said the pathologist, looking up to the gallery through floor to ceiling glass windows. The speaking switch was activated so they could converse easily, although it made their voices sound tinny. "It's exactly the same as Julie Andrews. The ring was lodged inside her." He nodded to a kidney-shaped bowl on the table behind him where even from up in the gallery, Rob could make out the dull sparkle. Four carats.

"It's definitely the same guy, then," confirmed Rob, feeling an odd sense of relief that the ring was there. Had it not been, it would have cast doubt on their entire theory. At least this guy was consistent, if nothing else. Patterns, as Tony had said.

"I would assume so. She's got dried blood and bruising on her inner thighs and some internal damage. I've taken swabs, but I wouldn't hold out much hope of any DNA."

"Condom?" asked Rob.

The pathologist nodded. "Yes, I can smell the lubricant on the latex. I'm sorry."

"What about her fingernails? Or on the tape?"

"The samples have already gone to the lab. If he's left any DNA on that duct-tape, we'll get it."

"Fingers crossed," said Rob.

"WHAT GOES INTO PLANNING A WEDDING?" Rob asked Yvette later that night. They were sitting in the lounge finishing off a bottle of red when he popped the question.

Amusement flickered across her face. "You want to start planning our wedding? But we don't even have a date yet."

He laughed. "No, although we should pick a date soon. I'm asking because of this case. Both girls were engaged to be married, and I think that's how he's finding them."

The amusement turned to irritation and then to fear. "You mean the Surrey Stalker?"

Rob paused. "Surrey Stalker? Christ, is that what they're calling him?"

She nodded. "It's in all the papers."

Rob felt the tension rise up his neck. Trust the media to label him, now he's probably gloating over his nickname. Well, hopefully it'll make him more reckless, more prone to mistakes.

Yvette bit her lip. "This stalker, this killer... he's targeting engaged girls?"

"Yeah." That information had been kept back from the press release, along with the rings. "Don't mention it to anyone, okay? It's not common knowledge."

She stared at him, then said slowly, "How does he know they're engaged?"

"That is what I'm trying to find out."

She nodded thoughtfully. "So, you want to know what goes into planning a wedding? There is the dress, obviously. That is the most important thing. A lot of thought goes into choosing it, because it must be perfect. Then there are the shoes, the hair, the accessories," she dropped her voice, "the wedding night lingerie."

Rob knew she was trying to provoke him, but he forced his mind to stay on the conversation.

"What about a wedding planner?"

She shrugged. "Not everyone has a wedding planner. Some people prefer to arrange it themselves. It's easy enough to book a venue, arrange catering, and invite the guests." She reached forward to grab her cigarette packet off the table. "If you're not doing anything too flamboyant."

Rob got the impression that's exactly the kind of wedding Yvette would want. Something simple and elegant, not too flamboyant. Despite her glamorous formative job, she didn't need to be the centre of attention, preferring to command the attention of one person, rather than a whole room. That's what had drawn him to her. Her ability to make him feel like the only man in the room.

He was taking mental notes. "Okay, what else?"

"There would be the flower arrangements, the bridal bouquet and the flowers in the church or wherever." She lit a cigarette. Rob watched the smoke escape from her mouth and felt an irresistible urge so do the same. One cigarette. How bad could that be? Yvette, sensing his craving, held the pack out to him. He almost took one, then shook his head. If he caved, he'd owe Luke fifty bucks.

She shrugged as if to say, 'Your loss,' and carried on talking. "Of course, there is the wedding cake, which would be made by a professional baker and to order. The catering for the reception, the band or DJ."

Rob rubbed his forehead. "Christ, there's a lot to it, isn't there?" He'd never pondered the depths of wedding arrangements before. No wonder people hired a planner. There were so many people to investigate, so many possibilities. For both the girls. Perhaps the information on their laptops would shed some light, narrow down their options.

She smirked and let out another stream of smoke.

"Of course."

10

"What about the rings?" Rob asked Mallory the next morning. He'd come in early and was standing beside the coffee machine waiting for the painfully slow drip-feed to fill up his pint-sized coffee mug. He brought his own in because he finished the paper cup sized coffees within three large gulps. It was shit coffee, but at least this way he got a decent caffeine hit, which didn't make it a completely useless endeavour.

"What about them?"

"Well, they must have been bought from somewhere? Do we know which jewellers they used?"

"I'll find out," said Mallory, finally cottoning on. He looked better than yesterday, but that wasn't saying much. Rob doubted any of them would feel completely normal until this case was over. The sun hadn't yet risen, but outside the window a couple of early-birds tweeted furiously. Only a handful of the team were in, including the boss who always seemed to arrive before anyone else, unless he had a meeting off-site.

Rob finally retrieved his coffee mug from under the overheated machine and went back to his desk.

"It's not the wedding planner." Luke marched over to Rob with a document in his hand. His jaw was clenched, and he seemed to be grinding his teeth. The hand holding the paper shook ever so slightly.

"Are you okay?" asked Rob, concerned.

"Withdrawals. I went from twenty a day to zero. I'm not sure this is good for my health."

"I hear you. I nearly caved yesterday, and this bloody case doesn't help." It was getting harder and harder to resist. This investigation was pushing them hard, the phone never stopped ringing, and the press were still camped out across the road. On top of it all, the DCI wanted results and Scotland Yard was breathing down their necks.

"Why isn't it the wedding planner?"

"Because Julie Andrews didn't have one. She was arranging the whole thing herself. Her fiancé said they'd reserved a room above a pub in Kew for the reception. The Greyhound, I believe it was. The ceremony was going to be held in the local church, and they were going to Scotland for their honeymoon."

"We can rule that out, then. What about the wedding dress? Any joy there?"

Luke pursed his lips. "I couldn't find any link to the dress on Sara's laptop, but Julie had bought an off-the-shelf number from a wedding shop in South Kensington and was having alternations done."

"A low-key affair, by all accounts," mused Rob. Julie and Justin were young, only a few years out of university, they didn't have the funds for an extravagant wedding. Unlike Sara and Gareth.

"Yes, makes you think it was the real deal."

Rob was inclined to agree, although just because someone had money, didn't mean they were any less in love.

"Maybe Sara's mother knows, or that friend of hers, Vivian, was it?"

"Yeah, I've got their numbers from Mallory. I'll get back to you on that."

"Actually, I think I'll go and see her mother," said Rob thoughtfully. "She might be able to shed some light on her daughter's movements."

"Right, we'll talk later." Luke strode off, flicking the piece of paper he was holding against the palm of his hand.

MRS. BAKSHI LIVED IN A SMALL, ex-council block in Surbiton. She'd moved to the area from Peterborough when her husband had died in order to be nearer her daughter. She was a petite, Indian woman in a flowing sari with a smudged red bhindi in the middle of her forehead. Once Rob had explained who he was and shown his warrant card, she'd given a little bow and beckoned for him to follow her into the apartment. It was cold inside, not made any warmer by the threadbare carpets and lack of heating. Obviously, her daughter's lucrative alliance hadn't filtered down to her yet.

"Please, sit."

Rob took a seat at the dining room table which took up half the lounge. She waited until he was comfortable then sat herself. "Are you here to talk about my Sara?"

Her eyes were filled with sadness, but there were no tears. Perhaps she'd already cried them all out and there were none left to fall.

"Yes, if you don't mind?"

She shook her head.

"Thank you." He composed his thoughts. "Firstly, I was wondering if you knew where Sara was having her wedding dress made?"

Grief flashed across the woman's face, but then it was gone

again. Just the sad eyes remained. "Yes, my friend was making it for her. It was a traditional wedding gown with an Indian twist. At least, that's what she liked to say. I suppose no one will ever get to wear it now." Her face fell.

"I'm so sorry for your loss." So, it wasn't the dressmaker either. One was custom-made, the other an off-the-shelf item. Another dead end.

Yet, the stalker was still targeting them somehow.

"What other preparations had Sara made for the wedding, do you know?"

Mrs. Bakshi thought for a moment. "Well, last week we went to that wedding show at London Olympia. I don't know if that's significant? They have various designers there, cakes, people toting venues, that sort of thing. We spent the day there, looking at the different stalls, getting ideas for the wedding."

A wedding which would now never happen.

"Did she engage with anyone, talk to any of the exhibitors?"

Sara's mother nodded. "Yes, of course. Lots of them. We took brochures. I've still got them somewhere, if you're interested?"

"That would be great." He felt the sizzle of anticipation. Was the wedding show the link? Could that be how the stalker was selecting his prey? It would be filled with unsuspecting girls searching for ideas for their own wedding. A perfect hunting ground.

He waited while Mrs. Bakshi went to get the flyers, then said his thanks and left the apartment block. Outside, he called Luke. While it was ringing, he turned his face up to the weak sun. It felt good after the cold, dark flat.

"There was a wedding show at Earl's Court Olympia last week. Let's look into it. It might be how he's finding them. Can you get a list of the exhibitors? I'll be back in the office in half an hour."

A slight pause. Rob knew what he was thinking. There'd be hundreds of them. "Sure, I'm on it." It was a long shot, granted, but they could start by focusing on the ones Sara and her mother spoke to. He told Luke to get hold of Justin King and ask him if Julie went to the wedding show.

The moment Rob walked into the station, Luke bellowed from across the room, "She did. She bloody did."

All faces turned to face him.

Rob fist-pumped the air. They'd finally got it. The connection between the two victims.

"Meeting," he yelled.

The team, desperate for a lead, didn't need asking twice. In a matter of seconds, they'd rallied around him. The air of expectancy was palpable.

"This had better be good," rasped DCI Lawrence, coming out of his office where he'd been holed up most of the day, shouting down the telephone. No one had dared disturb him.

"We've found the connection," began Rob, looking around at the delighted faces of his team. "It's the wedding expo at Earl's Court Olympia the weekend before last. Both girls were there, Julie on her own and Sara with her mother. So, someone at that exhibition noticed them, got their details and targeted them. Now he may have followed them home, but he couldn't have followed both, so I'm thinking they must have given him their details, their email address, phone number, something that he used to track them down at a later date."

There were several nods of agreement, including the DCI. "Makes sense."

"This is our first definite lead, so let's get a list of all those companies who exhibited and start working through it. We need to know which employees were at the fair, whether they took email addresses or phone numbers for marketing purposes, and so on."

"I've got the list." Luke raised his hand in the air.

The meeting broke up as officers congregated around Luke's desk. He allocated them each a sub-category of companies.

"Rob, a word." DCI nodded towards his office.

Rob followed him in. There was a spring in his step now that they had a connection.

"I've spent all day on the phone fielding calls from the press who as you know are particularly apt at putting two and two together. Two girls, two identical murders. We can't keep it hidden any longer. We're going to have to issue another statement.

"You mean *I'm* going to." Rob met the DCI's gaze.

Lawrence sighed, and rubbed his temples. He looked tired, which was out of character for him. Usually, he worked most of them under the table. Rob felt a flicker of concern. "Is there something else?"

The DCI nodded. "It's the Yard. They're insisting on sending that MIT over to assist with the case. I've begged for extra time, but they don't want to hear it.

At Rob's stricken look he raised a bushy eyebrow. "Two girls, Rob. Two bodies."

Rob sank into the chair opposite Lawrence's desk. He supposed it was inevitable really. A bona fide serial killer on the loose in west London, what did he expect? This case was snowballing and was now bigger than him.

"But, we've just got our first lead." He realized he sounded like a whinging schoolboy, so he snapped out of it. "By the time they get here, we'll have something definite to give them."

Lawrence squared his shoulders. "That's the spirit. The team will be arriving tomorrow morning, so you've got until the end of today to find us a name. If we can get surveillance on this guy, it's only a matter of time before we reel him in. We'll leave the Yard's murder squad with nothing to do except shuffle their paperwork."

Rob glanced at his watch. It was already ten a.m. He left

Lawrence's office and marched straight over to Mallory who he updated on the situation. Mallory's face dropped.

"I know, it's a bitch, but there's nothing we can do about it. We've got until the end of the day."

Luke, who'd overheard the hushed conversation, said, "We're moving as fast as we can."

Rob grimaced. "I know. Let me know if I can help."

CELESTE CAME out of the CCTV studio and blinked like a mole who'd just ventured above ground. She scanned the open-plan office.

"You looking for me?" called Rob who was back at the coffee machine. It was making a deep, groaning sound as it dripped away.

Celeste came over. "Yeah, we think we've got something."

He left his mug there and followed her back into her warren. It was warm and stuffy in the dimly lit room. He gazed at the screen in front of the empty chair in which she'd been sitting.

"This is from the CCTV camera outside Harrods in Knightsbridge at two-forty on Saturday afternoon. A female figure was frozen on the screen. Celeste leaned forward and pressed a button, the video continued with a sight whir. Rob recognized the woman as Sara Bakshi dressed in jeans and a striped T-shirt with gold lettering on the front. Stylish and attractive, she fit in perfectly with the elegant crowd on the Knightsbridge pavement.

"She leaves Harrod's and makes her way down Brompton Road towards Harvey Nicks. Shortly afterwards, a man in a hoodie follows her."

Rob stared at the screen without blinking. He didn't want to miss a thing. There! Less than a minute later, a tall, hooded man passed in front of the camera. The sun caught his cheekbone and while they couldn't see the front of his face, they could make out the shadow in his thin concave cheek and the smattering of a beard. His nose and the front of his face was too dark to make out.

"That's great. Well done. It's more than we've had until this point and we can confirm he's grown a beard."

"He could be trying to disguise himself, alter his appearance in case he gets caught on camera," suggested Celeste. "Maybe he's hoping to throw us off."

"If he insists on wearing that hoodie, he's easy enough to spot. Ironically, that's probably how we'll catch him."

"I'll keep going and see if any of the other cameras pick him up further down the street."

"What about inside Harrods?"

"I had a look at the main entrance feed but couldn't see him. I thought it best to continue down the pavement first, but I will check the other cameras in case he went inside. They have loads."

"Great. Can you make a digital copy of that image? One of the companies at the expo might recognize him. He could be one of their employees, or even a member of the Olympia staff."

"Sure thing, guv."

He went back to his desk, deep in thought. They were getting closer, he could feel it. The more the stalker escalated his activities the more exposed he was becoming. Now they had a profile shot. Granted, it wouldn't hold up in court, but perhaps someone would recognize him. He updated Luke and got him to email the digital still to the exhibitors.

By FIVE O'CLOCK, they still didn't have a name. The clock was ticking, and Rob was desperate for a cigarette. If he drank any more coffee he'd be sick. Maybe some fresh air would help. As he went downstairs he bumped into Luke looking sheepish.

"You didn't?" He snorted.

"No, but I'm about to." Luke looked like a man defeated.

"Thank God," breathed Rob. "I'll join you."

"Seriously?" Luke's face lit up.

"Yeah, I'm sure one won't hurt. It's been four fucking months."

They went downstairs, and Rob bought a packet from the newsagent on the corner. He felt like a naughty schoolboy as he pulled off the wrapper and offered the first one to Luke.

"Cheers." He took one with barely controlled excitement.

They lit up and inhaled deeply.

"Christ, I needed this." Rob tilted his head back and letting the smoke filter over his tongue and up into the moist afternoon air. The sporadic sun of the morning had disappeared, replaced by rapidly gathering clouds, heavy with rain. As far as Aprils go, this hadn't been a very good one.

Luke didn't reply, he was enjoying the moment.

After a long, pleasurable pause, Luke said, "I guess it was a draw."

Rob chuckled. "I can live with that."

"Any luck with the exhibitors yet?" Rob leaned against the side of the building.

"Not as yet," Luke replied. "We're almost halfway through the list. So far no one's recognised our guy, but several took email addresses for marketing purposes. Unfortunately, neither Julie nor Sara were on any of those lists."

"There's still time." Rob pulled on his cigarette for the last time and flicked the stub into the gutter where it sizzled out. "You're only halfway through the list, right?"

Luke nodded, then ground his cigarette into the pavement.

Rob repeated. "There's still time."

11

It was after midnight when Rob got home. The way he ached, you'd think he'd run a marathon. All he wanted to do was have a hot shower and collapse into bed. They'd worked every angle, called every company to see if anyone recognised the profile shot of their killer. No one had. He'd even spoken to HR at Earl's Court Olympia, and they couldn't shed any light. Rob had to wonder if perhaps one of the people they'd spoken to was in fact, their killer. How would they know? Tomorrow, he might send out the uniformed police to pay them a visit, armed with the photograph of their mystery stalker.

Tomorrow, the bloody MIT team would be there, and he'd be shoved aside. Not off the case, the DCI had assured him, but demoted. Ms. Maguire, who ticked all the right boxes, would be taking up the reins. Well, he hoped she could handle it. His team had worked their asses off and he couldn't imagine they'd be too happy with a new guvnor in the building.

To make matters worse, Yvette was giving him the silent treatment again. He'd called her twice and left messages, but she hadn't answered or rung him back. Granted, he'd been on the phone all evening, but he could see there were no missed calls. He'd also given another press conference with the efficient Vicky at his side, where he outlined the details of the second murder. Like before, he'd kept it short, only the facts, and asked that if anyone had any information to get in touch. Then Vicky had invited him out for a drink, but he'd politely declined, even though he was dying for one. She wasn't his type and he didn't want to lead her on. Yvette aside, he was too rough around the edges for someone like her.

The last appeal hadn't turned anything up in the way of leads and the calls had trickled off. He had no doubt Twickenham would be besieged with a fresh bout of callers over the next twenty-four hours and there was always a chance someone had seen something, but he wasn't betting on it. Both murders had occurred in isolated locations off the beaten track where there were no lights or cameras, and no pedestrians. In other words, no way of noticing someone assaulting a woman in the bushes.

He went upstairs to find the bedroom door locked from the inside. Yvette was making her disapproval noted. Sighing, he went back downstairs. It would be the couch again, although he was too tired to care. After a shower and some cold gluten-free pizza that tasted like cardboard, which he found in a box on the kitchen table, he hit the sack.

"I'M MOVING OUT," Yvette announced the next morning as he was about to leave. She wasn't dressed for work yet, but then she had an hour still, while he liked to get in early. Her shift began at ten, and she liked to languish at home and bathe, dress slowly and do her make-up before catching the Piccadilly Line into Knightsbridge.

"What do you mean?" Rob stopped in his tracks. The front

door was open letting in a blast of cold morning air, so he shut it again.

"You're never home," she said, pouting sexily. "I don't want to live by myself, especially not with a killer around. It's scary. Besides, you never answer your phone."

"I'm sorry. You know I'm busy."

"Well, you know I'm home alone. So, I'm going to stay with Naomi until I figure out what to do about us."

He could tell by her voice she was serious. This wasn't the usual strop and sulk. She really meant it.

"There's nothing wrong with us." He came towards her. She didn't move away but didn't react either. He touched her arm. "I mean it, we're fine. It's just this case, once it's over..."

"When it's over, it will be too late." Her lovely oval eyes clouded over.

"No, it doesn't have to be. I promise I'll make it up to you." He was pleading now. How could she walk out at such a crucial time? Didn't she know how much stress he was under? Didn't she care?

"There will always be another case, Robert. Like you say, this is your job. I don't want to be with a policeman anymore. It's lonely."

That gave him pause. She was right. There would always be another case. It's what drove him, and if he were honest, he liked catching killers. He'd never change, never be the type of man she wanted him to be. His heart sank. Was this the end, then? Where they breaking up? He took a deep breath. "Maybe you're right. Maybe we should take a break." He gazed at her lovely face and felt an overwhelming sense of sadness. "But stay in touch, okay. I want to know you're safe."

She turned around without replying and marched upstairs. Had she been waiting for a reaction, for him to beg her to stay? He wasn't sure, he couldn't tell. Why were relationships so fucking complicated? He wondered briefly if he should go after her, then decided against it. It wouldn't change anything. He couldn't stay, he had to go and meet DCI Maguire and he didn't want to create a bad first impression. With a sigh, he left the house, closing the door softly behind him.

THE STALKER WATCHED Yvette leave the house. She was pulling a suitcase on four wheels, like the ones you took when flying to Europe, light and easy to wheel around large airports and on and off trains. Was she moving out?

He watched from the comfort of a greasy spoon café a short distance up the road. The windows were grubby, and the air smelled of fried food, but it made for a great vantage point. He was pretty sure she wouldn't be coming in here. Not her style.

He watched as she wheeled the suitcase past. She looked sad. Trouble in paradise? Because of this case? Because of him? He shivered with glee. The press were beside themselves, splashing photographs of his latest victims all over the newspapers and on the TV. The police were appealing for information, they even had a dedicated hot-line for information on him. And Bridget had said he'd never amount to much.

Well, look at me now.

Yvette paused and consulted her phone. She must be waiting for a taxi or an Uber. Her hand held the device while the other scrolled. She had long, elegant fingers, and her nails glistened with red polish. She twisted her left hand ever so slightly, so it caught the light.

It was then he spotted the ring.

12

Jo Maguire was a five-foot-ten blonde bombshell. Rob paused outside Lawrence's fishbowl office and watched as she laughed with him like they were old friends. He frowned, she'd won over his gruff boss already. He'd known Lawrence for three years and still hadn't made him laugh like that. But then he wasn't a five-foot ten blonde bombshell.

He couldn't see her face, but from the back she looked sensational in figure-hugging denim jeans and a white blouse.

Lawrence spotted him and gestured for him to join them. Rob exhaled, squared his shoulders and prepared for battle.

"This is DCI Maguire, from Scotland Yard."

"Please, call me Jo." She held out a hand. Her handshake was firm, but soft. She was equally as sensational from the front. Her face was clear and devoid of make-up, yet she still looked good. There was a smidgeon of gloss on her lips, but that was it, a small nod to vanity. And she smelled good too. A waft of something sweet like caramel floated over to him.

"Pleased to meet you, Jo," he said, following instructions.

Lawrence nodded in approval. "This is the SIO on the case, DI Rob Miller. I'll let him fill you in."

She turned to Lawrence and smiled. "Thanks, Sam. I appreciate the support."

Sam? Now that was a first. Lawrence didn't meet his eye. "Don't mention it. Now if you'll excuse me, I have a nine o'clock meeting across town."

Rob gestured to the round table in Lawrence's office that was reserved for internal meetings. "We may as well take a seat and I'll bring you up to speed."

He watched as she eased herself into the chair, swinging one of her long legs across the other, then leaning back to study him.

"I hope you're not upset about us barging in like this," she said with a light-hearted smile, but her eyes, a deep, clear blue weren't laughing. "Orders from above."

Rob shrugged. "It can't be helped." He wasn't going to tell her it was fine when it wasn't. "But that doesn't mean we can't work together," he added diplomatically.

She grinned. "I was hoping you'd say that."

Rob had to admit, she had a disarming smile, and the little dimple in her left cheek was endearing. Despite himself, he liked her. "How much do you know?"

"Most of it," she said without a beat. "I've read all the files. I know about the rings," her forest eyes met his over the table. "Good move not mentioning that to the press."

"Orders from above."

The dimple appeared. "I've seen your profile shot of the killer, and I've read the notes on the wedding expo. Good work, by the way."

"Thanks. Unfortunately, we didn't find anything. No one recognized him."

"Have you considered that he might have been one of the people you spoke to?"

He met her gaze. "Of course. I was going to send uniform out today to do some follow-ups. If they spot anyone matching our profile shot, they'll let us know."

"Good idea." She paused, thinking. "Otherwise, you've got a dozen people working on CCTV?"

He couldn't tell if she thought that was a good or a bad thing.

"Yes, they're tracing the two victims' last movements, when we know the stalker was following them. It's a full-time job."

"Hey, I'm not mocking it. I've done my time in the video studio." She held up her hands. "And I agree, it's worth the manpower."

Well, what do you know? She wasn't what he'd expected, although he wasn't quite sure what that was. A university graduate, perhaps, on a fast-track career path to the top? She looked like she'd worked her way up, her accent was fairly strong, not softened by private schools and universities, and while she was congenial, there was a strength he saw in her eyes, that impressed him. He got the impression she didn't suffer fools gladly.

He learned that first hand when Mallory bounded in and not noticing them sitting in the DCI's office, said, "When's the teacher's pet arriving?"

"Excuse me," she said to Rob. He watched as she stood up and walked to the door. Mallory paled when he saw her. She smiled sweetly and said, "I don't believe we've met. I'm Jo Maguire, teacher's pet, and you are...?"

Rob couldn't help but chuckle. He followed her out and made the introductions. There were just five of them in since it was only eight fifteen. The working day officially began at nine, and since they'd all worked late the night before, Rob didn't think many would make it in before then.

"This is DI Gary Stewart," she said as a broad-shouldered man with a thick neck and a crooked nose strode in. He had the heavy-set features of a boxer and looked like a man who knew how to handle himself. "He's my right-hand man."

Gary nodded around the room but didn't speak. More like bodyguard, thought Rob. The strong, silent type.

"Where shall we plonk ourselves?" asked Jo, deferring once again to Rob. He appreciated it, but it wasn't necessary. She was the senior detective and could quite rightly take control any way she wanted. It meant a lot that she was treading lightly.

"There are a couple of empty desks over there, and more in the next room," Rob said. "How many of you are there?"

"Twenty in my team, but only Gary and I will be based here. These two desks will do fine."

He nodded. That was a relief. At least they weren't going to get flooded with newcomers. Just then his mobile rang. He glanced at the screen, it was forensics.

"Any news?" he said immediately.

He listened for a moment, then fist-pumped the air. "Yes!"

Jo's head swung around. "What?"

We have a partial print on the duct-tape, and it doesn't belong to the victim.

"Can we run it?" asked Jo.

"I'll get on it right now," said Mallory, determined to make up for his previous faux pas. Half an hour later, they still didn't have an ID.

"Whoever he is, isn't in the database," said Mallory, putting on his hang-dog face. "It doesn't get us anywhere."

"It will once we get a suspect," said Jo, optimistically.

If we get a suspect, thought Rob.

"Let's go grab a coffee," Jo said to Rob once everyone was in and introductions had been made. "I'm buying."

They crossed the road and went to the local Italian coffee shop. There was a large sign advertising *Lavazza*, by the door. "Perfect. I can't stand that stuff in your machine," she complained, rolling her eyes. "I don't know how you handle it."

They got their coffees, a cappuccino for her and a double-shot Americano for him. He may as well make the most of it.

"I've been thinking about this stalker," she began, wrapping both her hands around the paper cup. "Have you done a psychological profile on him?"

"Not officially." Rob told her about his mate, Tony. She knew of him. "That's great, but we need something official, something in writing. If we use it to help catch this guy, it'll be admissible in court."

She was already thinking about the prosecution, while he was just concerned with catching the fucker.

"Sure, I'll ask Tony to write something up. It'll have to go through the official channels, though." Tony would need to be paid for his time. Would the budget stretch that far? Profiling was gaining popularity, but it wasn't there yet, not in the U.K. anyway and many considered it a waste of resources. Clearly, not Jo.

"Absolutely. I'll clear it with DCI Lawrence. In the meantime, why don't you tell me what you know?"

"This guy has issues with marriage."

"Who doesn't, right?" She tucked a wispy strand of hair that had escaped her ponytail behind her ear.

Rob grinned, but continued with his train of thought. "He targets engaged women, then kills them before the wedding."

"Days before?" Jo was serious now, her gaze fixed on his face.

"Yeah, or maybe weeks," confirmed Rob. "He stalks them beforehand, gets to know their routines, where they work, where they play, then he chooses his spot, which is usually isolated and devoid of people, and waits."

Jo sipped her coffee thoughtfully. Froth landed on her upper lip, drawing his eye. He watched, slightly bemused, as she licked it off.

"So, we can assume he was jilted once before, and the girl he loved got engaged to someone else?"

"Yup, that's the current theory. Then he loses it. He can't handle the fact she's going to marry someone else. He watches her every move, until one day he threatens her, it goes too far, and he kills her."

Jo stared at him for a moment, then said, "It would be great if we could find out who 'she' is? The original victim, the one who started all this."

Rob sighed. "We tried, we combed the cold case files for women who'd been raped and strangled, or even one of the two. No luck. It was either a dead end or the pattern didn't match."

"What about cases where the perpetrator was arrested?" asked Jo.

Rob frowned. "You mean they could have got the wrong guy?"

She pursed her lips. "It happens."

Rob was silent as he let her words percolate. Could they have missed something? "I suppose it is possible," he began.

"I'll get my guys to look into it," she said deftly. "Your team has enough on their plate."

LATER THAT AFTERNOON, Jo perched on Rob's desk. She had a very familiar way about her, she seemed to break down barriers without you even realising. Most of his team were under her spell already, including himself, he acknowledged wryly.

"My team might have found something," she said in her broad Yorkshire accent.

"What's that?"

"Four years ago, in Kent, a girl was found dead on the beach near Deal. She'd been raped and murdered."

"Was she strangled?" asked Rob, hardly daring to hope.

Jo nodded. "It was messy. According to the coroner's report, she took a while to die. There were bruises and burn marks covering her body. He went to town with this one, Rob, and took his time doing it."

"Could she have been his first?" wondered Rob.

"That's what I was thinking? Fancy a trip to the seaside?"

13

For once the sky wasn't covered in clouds, but it was blustery, particularly down at the beach. Jo's blonde hair whipped around her face, threatening to be torn loose from its binding.

"This is where she was found." PC Warren shouted to be heard above the wind. They were standing beside a concrete groyne, which began halfway up the beach and disappeared into the sea like a rigid serpent's tail. It ran oblique to the shoreline catching and trapping the shingle as it washed up onto the shore. "I was the first officer on the scene and I'll never forget it. Poor lass. She was naked too."

Rob frowned. "What? No clothes on at all?"

The PC shook his head. "None, whatsoever, although some of her body was covered by shingle, but whether it was intentional or not, we have no idea. It could have been from the longshore drift." He nodded down the coastline.

"Who found her?" Rob squinted against the wind, which made his eyes water.

"A woman taking an early morning stroll. Come on, let's go inside. DCI Becker is waiting for us." He led them up the beach and onto a wide pavement where wooden benches had been positioned every hundred yards or so to enable people to sit and watch the gulls dip and hover over the sea or admire the Kent coastline. Interspersed between the benches were lamp posts festooned with colourful hanging baskets. Across the road, a line of pastel-coloured beachfront apartments, shops and cafés created a picturesque seaside façade.

They went into a small café with faded rose-patterned curtains made by some long-ago well-meaning proprietor and an assortment of mismatched tables and chairs. Shabby chic, Rob thought it was called but he wasn't sure. The glass cabinet at the front housed a delicious selection of pastries, cakes and muffins, and he suddenly realised how hungry he was. Jo, however, moved directly towards a table at the back where a grey-haired man in a khaki fleece sat watching them. In front of him was an untouched cup of coffee. Sustenance would have to wait. Rob joined them, along with PC Warren who made the introductions.

"DCI Becker, this is DCI Maguire and DC Miller from London. They're here about Bridget Kane."

"Retired DCI," said Becker standing briefly to shake hands. "Please, sit down."

As soon as they had, a waitress appeared to take their order. Rob asked for a large Americano, which he hoped would buoy him up for a while, and Jo ordered a latte. PC Warren declined.

"Now, what can I do for you?"

"You could outline the case for us." Jo offered up a dimpled smile. "Just so we have the facts straight."

The retired detective warmed to her, and even offered a smile in return, which judging by PC Warren's surprised expression, didn't happen very often. "Of course. Of course. It was a long time ago, but I remember it as if it were yesterday. Bridget Kane was twenty-one years old when she was killed. I was at her twenty-first birthday party."

"You knew the victim?" asked Jo, surprised.

He nodded sadly. "Yes, I was friends with her father. He passed away a few years ago, poor sod. Cancer. Wouldn't be surprised if it wasn't the shock of his daughter's death that did it."

Jo gave a sympathetic nod.

He continued. "As PC Warren has told you, she was found over there on the beach beside the groyne, stark naked. She'd been raped and strangled." He shook his head. "It was a tragedy. The whole town came out in mourning. No one could believe it. There'd never been such a violent crime in Deal before and there hasn't been since, as far as I know."

"Except for that decapitated head that washed up last year," pointed out PC Warren helpfully.

Becker glared at him, and he went back to studying his hands.

"I believe you made an arrest." Rob steered him back to the case.

"Yeah, she'd been dating this guy called Ron Studley, a local lad. He was a bit of shit, if you'll excuse my French. Always in trouble at school, arrested once or twice for disturbing the peace, that sort of thing. I hauled him in once for smashing a chair over his stepfather's head. He said the guy deserved it." He sighed. "He had a temper on him, but I never took him for the murdering kind. Shows how wrong I was."

"What evidence did you have on him?" Jo asked, beating Rob to it.

"That was the thing, the evidence was irrefutable. Bridget's clothes were found in the rubbish bin outside his house and her DNA was in the boot of his car where he'd transported the body."

"She wasn't killed on the beach?" Jo frowned.

"No, not according to forensics. She'd been raped and strangled in a field judging by the grass stains on the back of her heels and elbows and the blades of grass in her hair. She may also have been dragged across the field to the car, before he drove her to the beach and dumped her body."

"Why would he do that?" asked Rob. "He could just as easily have left her body on the field to be found?"

Becker shrugged. "Who knows? Maybe he was buying time? According to the pathologist, she died at least twelve hours before she was found. That puts the time of death at around seven o'clock the previous evening. Ron said he was home alone watching TV, but no one could vouch for him."

"What about the burn marks?" asked Jo.

"Those were inflicted prior to her death," Becker said with a small shake of his head. "Poor lass must have suffered horribly."

"So, he tortured her before he raped and strangled her." Rob said more to himself than to anyone else. Jo was watching him.

"What are you thinking?"

"I'm thinking this was personal. He was upset, he wanted to hurt her."

She nodded. "I tend to agree. He was punishing her."

Becker leaned forward and said conspiratorially, "Her fiancé admits they had an argument earlier that day but denied anything to do with her murder. He claimed he hadn't seen her since then."

"What did they argue about?" Jo wanted to know.

He straightened up again. "To be honest, I can't quite remember. I think it had something to do with her parents. They never did like him much. Didn't think he was good enough for their little girl. Turns out they were right." He nodded towards the manila folder lying on the table. "It'll be in the report."

"Can we take this with us?" Jo gave him another smile.

He pushed the folder over to her. "It's all yours."

They finished their coffees and Becker pushed his chair back, scraping the legs against the floor. "I hope it helps you. I believe you have something similar up in London?"

Rob didn't meet his gaze. "There are definite similarities."

"Well, Ron Studley is serving a life sentence at Whitemoor which makes for a pretty decent alibi." He chuckled at his little joke.

As they walked out of the café, Rob asked, "Were there any other suspects in the case? Anyone who may have harboured a grudge against Bridget, for some reason?"

"Are you saying we got the wrong guy?" Becker stopped walking and his expression darkened. He didn't like to be second-guessed. PC Warren edged away from them towards the front door. Becker squared up to Rob. "The evidence was indisputable. Her clothes were found in his bin, there was grass and hair in the boot of his car and he didn't have an alibi for the time of the murder. It was him all right. The jury agreed. They took less than an hour to convict him."

Jo put a hand on the retired detective's arm. "That's not what we're saying," she said softly. "DC Miller is just covering all the bases. I'm sure you asked yourself the same questions at the time."

Becker grunted. "Of course we did, but we had to prosecute based on the evidence."

"Which was pretty indisputable," Jo reiterated, showing her dimple and letting Becker hold the door open for her.

"Is THERE anyone you can't charm?" asked Rob, as he turned onto the A20 towards the motorway back to London.

Jo grinned. "It does come in handy sometimes, besides haven't you heard, you catch more flies with honey?"

"Maybe you do," he mumbled, causing her grin to turn into a chuckle. "It's never quite worked for me."

"Perhaps you're not sweet enough." She was probably right.

Smooth FM played softly in the background and Rob, feeling more relaxed than he had in a long time, concentrated on the road ahead while Jo read silently through the case file.

"There's a couple of things that don't make sense." She glanced at him.

"Yeah?" He turned down the volume.

"For starters, why would Ron say he was home alone during the time of the murder? If he'd done it, surely he'd have come up with a better alibi than that?"

"Hmm... You have a point." It was rather lame as far as alibis went. Usually the perpetrator made sure someone had seen or could vouch for them before or after the murder to give their alibi some credibility. Rob apparently saw no one the whole evening and freely admitted it.

"Also, like you pointed out, why kill her in a field then transport the body to the beach? It's only going to provide more evidence for the police to find. The beach is exposed and highly visible. It's risky, even though it would have been dark by then. The body was much more likely to be found there, whilst the field, judging by this report, would have been fairly isolated."

"That did strike me as strange." Rob was glad she'd questioned it too. Why not leave her in the secluded field? What was the thinking behind the beach?

Jo continued, "And disposing of her clothes in his own rubbish bin? That seems a bit too obvious, even for a first-time criminal."

"Are you thinking he was set up?" Rob indicated and pulled into the left-hand lane, so he could ponder this in more detail.

She sighed. "I don't know, but he could have been. Think about it. If our killer wanted to get off scot-free, how better to do it than to frame someone else?"

Rob met her gaze. "And what better person to frame than the man who stole his girl from him?"

"Exactly."

It made sense.

"I think we should check it out, don't you?"

"Definitely." Rob turned his attention back to the front. "Let's pay Ron Studley a visit tomorrow morning and see what he has to say for himself."

14

It was a long drive back to Richmond, so they stopped at a service station on the M20 to grab a bite to eat and some more coffee. By this stage, Rob was ravenous. He practically inhaled a McDonald's burger before she'd even unwrapped hers.

Laughing, she shook her head. "Low blood sugar?"

He grinned, feeling better already. Jo, not surprisingly, was really easy to talk to and Rob found himself opening up about things he hadn't talked about in years. It turned out she had a degree in Psychology from Bristol University, which might explain it, but he was impressed nonetheless. It was far more than he could say for himself.

"I messed about a bit after school," he told her, while she ate. "Did some odd jobs, travelled a little, but then I started going off the rails. I was just bored, I guess. I began drinking heavily, got into a few bar fights with sleaze balls, I couldn't stand the way they behaved. Then my uncle suggested I join the police force. At first, I thought he was crazy, what would they want with a lout like me, right? But he wouldn't let up, so I got used to the idea and eventually signed up. After a couple of years in uniform, I applied to the criminal investigation department." He smiled. "I liked the idea of wearing my own clothes."

She finished her mouthful, then took a sip of her coke. "Have you always lived in Richmond?" she asked. He liked that she wasn't fussy about food. Yvette would never touch a McDonald's burger, fries, and a coke. She'd rather starve. It didn't make for very fun date nights.

"No, I was originally based in North London, but I got transferred here at the beginning of last year after I became a DI. They had an opening and I thought the change might do me good."

"And did it?"

"Yes." He thought he'd shared enough. "How about you? What made you decide to become a detective?"

There was a slight pause while she chewed the last of her burger. Then she said, "My sister went missing when we were kids. There was an extensive search, the whole village turned out to help, but they never found her."

"Christ, I'm sorry. I had no idea." He felt bad for asking.

She smiled sadly. "That's okay. It was a long time ago, nearly twenty years now, but I guess I've always had this burning desire to find out what had happened to her."

"And did you?"

She shook her head. "Not yet."

"Is that why you studied psychology?" He knew his mate Tony had gone into the field because he'd wanted to better understand the bi-polar disorder that had consumed his mother. Perhaps Jo needed to understand how someone could have taken her sister?

"It was part of it, but the workings of the human mind always fascinated me, so I figured it was as good a degree as any. My parents always wanted me to go to university. Then, after I graduated, I decided to use what I knew to catch killers, so I signed up to the Met's fast-track recruitment programme, and five years later, here I am."

So, his first instinct had been correct, although he'd been wrong about her being the teacher's pet. She worked hard, he could see that, and deserved the rank she'd achieved. That would put her at roughly twenty-eight. A year younger than him. "What about family?" he asked her. "Do you ever want to get married, have your own kids?"

"Sure," she gave him an odd look. "When the time is right. How about you?"

He shrugged. "I don't know if kids are on the cards for me." At the moment, he didn't even know if he was still in a relationship. Yvette had studiously ignored his texts and phone calls and wasn't returning his messages. Perhaps he'd go over to her sister's tonight and try to talk to her. He didn't like the way they'd left things. It felt wrong.

"Well, you never know." She smiled, and got up, taking her coke with her. "We'd better make a move else we'll never get back."

BACK AT THE STATION, Rob called a meeting and told his team what they'd discovered in Kent. "We don't know that it's related, yet," he told them, "but Jo and I are going to Whitemoor tomorrow to have a chat to this Ron Studley."

"Good idea," barked DCI Lawrence. "But let's keep this under wraps for now. We don't want to step on any toes. This man was tried and convicted for the murder of Bridget Kane so we're going to have to come up with some pretty compelling evidence before we say otherwise."

"Gotcha." Rob was in complete agreement. Retired DCI Becker wouldn't look too kindly on them opening the case again. He'd staked his career on that conviction.

"Any news on the CCTV footage?" he asked Celeste.

She shook her head. "Nothing new, guv."

"What about the wedding expo?"

Luke also shook his head. "We've got officers armed with the profile shot going around to all the companies, but so far nothing."

"Okay, keep at it." He looked at Mallory. "What about their laptops?"

"We've made a list of Julie's wedding contacts, as well as Sara's but so far there are no other crossovers. I think the expo is still our best bet."

"Right, thanks everyone."

IT WAS GONE eight when Rob next saw Jo. Her ash-blonde hair had successfully escaped its confines and more of it was falling around her face than was left in the band. There were faint smudges of mascara underneath her eyes, and the lip gloss had long since disappeared. She looked tired, but also cute and dishevelled.

"Any luck?" Rob slung his rucksack over his shoulder. He knew she'd gone to see a criminal profiler when they'd got back, and it had been a pretty long meeting by the looks of things. In the end, they'd gone with someone she'd used before and who the courts knew, rather than Tony. Secretly, he suspected she didn't want anyone who he had a connection with, as it might affect the prosecution. One thing he'd learned about her, was that she was always thinking ahead.

She stifled a yawn. "Yeah, it was very useful. I see everyone's left for the day." Her eyes met his. "Do you want to get a drink and we can go over it?"

Rob was tempted, but he needed to see Yvette who had now turned off her phone completely. After calling her sister, Naomi, he knew she was working the late shift tonight, and would come off at nine when the store closed, and he wanted to be there to meet her after work. It was important they talk.

"I'm sorry, I've got plans tonight." He was intrigued by what the profiler had come up with and if he were honest, he would have liked to have had a drink with Jo. She was good company. "Can we take a rain check?"

"Sure." If she was disappointed, she didn't show it. "We can go through it tomorrow. Have a good evening."

Rob said goodbye and left the office, just as she sank into her chair and switched on her computer. For Jo Maguire, the day was not over yet.

HARRODS, which took up a whole block of prime Knightsbridge real estate, was lit up like a fairy castle. Despite it being almost nine o'clock, Brompton Road was packed with people. There was a constant flow of shoppers being ushered out of the majestic building by eagle-eyed security guards. Rob stood on the corner under the tube sign and waited for Yvette to emerge. When she didn't come out, he went inside and asked at the cosmetics department where she was. Her supervisor, an elegant middle-aged woman who wore too much make-up, said she'd got off early and had gone for drinks with some of the others at Harvey Nicks. By her wistful tone, Rob got the impression she'd much rather be there than cashing up the till.

Harvey Nichols, also a familiar fixture in Knightsbridge, was the closest thing to competition that Harrods had, and sported a very fashionable cocktail bar on the fifth floor. Rob knew it well, having met Yvette there several times when they had first got together.

It was only a short walk away, and he emerged from the lift on the fifth floor less than ten minutes later. He spotted Yvette and her work colleagues immediately. They were sitting on the plush orange sofas against the windows, laughing and drinking. He felt a momentary flash of annoyance that she didn't seem to be as concerned by their current relationship crisis as he was. He recognized one or two of her colleagues, but there was a tall, bald man sitting next to her, that he did not know. The man was offering her a taste of his cocktail, and Rob frowned as Yvette put her scarlet lips around the straw and sucked.

Rob approached the table. Yvette spotted him and abruptly let the straw pop out of the corner of her mouth. Her eyes widened.

"Hello," Rob said, without smiling. "I thought I'd come and surprise you."

Yvette stood up. The man next to her looked up in interest, he had very arched eyebrows. Her girlfriends stopped talking. "Rob, why don't you join us?" Yvette purred, beckoning to him to come and sit next to her.

He shook his head. "Can I have a word?"

She excused herself and glided over to him. The smile had vanished from her face. "You might have given me some warning," she hissed. "You've embarrassed me in front of my friends."

"So, I need to warn you before I see you now, do I? Is that so you don't get caught with other men?"

Her eyes narrowed. "What are you talking about?"

"Him." Rob nodded towards the man with the cocktail.

"Oh, please. Don't be ridiculous. That's Simon. He's new and as gay as they come. Just look at him."

Rob studied the bald man who'd been sitting next to Yvette. His pale pink shirt was open at the neck showing a silver chain. Apart from his bald head, or perhaps to make up for it, he had a millennial-style beard and sported a trendy pair of black-rimmed spectacles. His legs were crossed in an effeminate manner and the hand that held the cocktail was pale and elegant with long, slender fingers.

Rob breathed a sigh of relief. "Sorry, I overreacted. I thought he was coming onto you."

She shrugged petulantly. "Would you care?"

He took her arm. "Of course, I care. I love you. You know that."

She shook her head.

"Please come home. I miss you."

Yvette gazed at him for a long moment, then she shook her head. "No, Robert. I'm having fun with my friends tonight. I don't want to come home."

He tried to embrace her, but she pulled away. He sighed. "We need to talk. We have to sort this out. I don't like it when there's conflict between us and I don't like it when you're not there."

Her lips went up in a smirk. "Ah, so now you know how I feel every night."

"It's not every night," he snapped, feeling the old anger return. She was being totally unreasonable. "It's only when I have a case on, and this is an important one. Why can't you see that?"

"I do see it," she said sulkily. "You always have a case on, and when you don't, you wish you did. You'd rather be catching criminals than home with me."

He released her arm. "Now, it's you who's being ridiculous."

She spun on her heel and he got a whiff of her perfume. It made him weak with longing. "Please, Yvette..."

She turned back, a scornful look on her face. "No, Robert. I need time to think this through. I'm not sure you're what I want anymore. I'm sorry."

She went back to her friends.

THE STALKER WATCHED as Yvette said goodbye to her friends and left Harvey Nichols. She was a little tipsy, he could tell by the way she teetered gently on her heels. He wondered if he should take her now. It would be so easy. Her senses were dulled, she was vulnerable. All he had to do was get her alone.

But no, it wasn't the right moment. It wasn't perfect.

He followed her at a distance, hoodie pulled up and head bent down to avoid the street lights and the cameras. He knew they were looking for him, it was obvious. He was currently on every police officer's most-wanted list. And London was littered with CCTV cameras, not only on the street, but outside shops and department stores, in parking lots and even on buses. There was no privacy anymore.

It was her fiancé, Detective Inspector Rob Miller, who was in charge of the case. He'd seen him on television again last night, informing the public about the rape and murder of Sara Bakshi in Richmond Park. There was quite a hoo-ha about it. Richmond Park, that peaceful idyll where families let their children play and dog-walkers ambled at leisure was a safe-haven no more. Now, it was tainted by blood. Sara's blood. People were scared to walk there alone, particularly after dark.

He shivered in excitement. Sometimes he couldn't quite believe he'd done that. He'd created this atmosphere of fear and panic. Him.

And *she'd* said he'd never amount to much.

They'd even given him a nickname, like all infamous serial killers. *The Surrey Stalker*. The hairs on his arms prickled in anticipation. It really was too good to be true.

He watched as Yvette went into a newsagent and bought a packet of cigarettes and a diet coke. She stood unsteadily on the pavement and lit one, inhaling deeply, clutching it between her red-painted nails. That diamond ring, that symbol of her alliance to *him*, flashed in the streetlights. She was an attractive woman. The stalker was looking forward to making her... making *him*... pay.

Yvette hailed a cab and leaned over to give the driver directions. He watched the way her skirt rode up the back of her thighs. Slut. It was designed to make men salivate, long for what they couldn't have. Despite himself, he grew hard, and rubbed himself to ease the ache. He was weak, like all men, but he was also powerful, and in those dark, secluded moments when his hands squeezed around his victims' necks, he redeemed himself. The cabbie nodded, and she opened the back door and climbed in.

The stalker melted into the shadows. He didn't need to follow her for he knew where she was going. "Soon," he whispered to himself as he watched the black cab drive away. "Soon it will be your turn."

15

Rob got to work early thanks to a restless night where he'd been plagued with disturbing thoughts about Yvette and the sobering fact that his relationship might well and truly be over. He glanced at DCI Lawrence's office, a glass bubble within the office, and saw that it was still in darkness. He raised an eyebrow. That had to be a first.

Not in the mood for crappy drip-fed coffee, he'd stopped at Starbucks and bought himself a grande double-shot Americano and as an afterthought, an almond croissant. He was just wiping the crumbs from his mouth when DCI Sam Lawrence marched in, purposeful and efficient, despite it being only ten past eight in the morning. His boss seemed surprised to see him there.

"Morning, Rob. What are you doing sitting in the dark? You got a new lead or something?"

Like there had to be a work-related reason for his early start.

"No, not yet. I couldn't sleep so I decided to come in."

Lawrence gave him a long look. "Case getting to you?"

"Nah, nothing like that. Just a bout of insomnia, that's all. Too much caffeine. I'll probably sleep like a baby tonight."

"Right." His boss's gaze dropped to the Starbucks cup on Rob's desk, then back up to his face again. He wasn't buying it. Rob shifted in his chair. The DCI had a way of making him feel uncomfortable at the best of times.

"You and Jo off to Whitemoor today?"

"Yeah, soon as she gets in."

"Good. Good. How are you getting on with her?" Lawrence paused at the entrance to his office, briefcase in hand.

Rob pursed his lips. "She's a professional. I've got no complaints."

"Glad to hear it. I thought she was very nice myself. A good copper, too. Excellent attention to detail, judging by her reports."

Rob didn't reply. He didn't know about her attention to detail, but he did know she was easy to be with, and sharp as a button, always one step ahead. Her instincts were spot-on, an important factor in detective work because sometimes your gut was all you had to go on.

"I'll let you get on." Lawrence pushed open his office door and switched on the light. The bubble illuminated giving Rob a perfect view of his pristine office. There were blinds to block out the rest of the office, but the DCI hardly ever used them. Rob suspected it was because he secretly liked to feel like he was part of the team, despite being the one assigned to watch over them. He wondered what that would be like, being in charge. It must be quite a heady feeling, calling all the shots. But then there was the political side too, the fielding of press calls, the schmoozing with the powers that be, all the stuff Rob wasn't very good at.

He turned his attention back to the folder on his desk. Ron Studley. Becker had been right about Ron being a trouble-maker in his youth. He'd been suspended from school on numerous occasions, once because he'd threatened a teacher using a fire extinguisher as a weapon, all because the teacher had given him detention. He'd had several warnings about brawling and one drunk and disorderly charge, and it was clear he had a temper, but they were all minor transgressions, nothing to indicate he harboured murderous tendencies. Then he met Bridget and he'd calmed down, or so it seemed. There were no mentions of any misdemeanours in his file from 2015 onwards. It appeared that Ron Studley had turned over a new leaf. He was attending college in the evenings, even though he worked as a mechanic in a local garage during the day. So, he was trying to better himself.

Was that Bridget's influence? She worked as a marketing manager for a Canterbury firm selling organic cosmetics. Maybe he wanted her to be proud of him, or maybe she realised his potential. Either way, he didn't strike Rob as a torturous killer.

He put the question to Jo as they drove along the M25 to Whitemoor. Once again, she was in the passenger seat, the same manila case folder open on her lap.

"I tend to agree with you," she said with a firm nod of her head. "Ron Studley had reformed. Why would he suddenly go on the rampage and torture, rape and murder his fiancé, the woman he loved? He'd never laid a hand on her before. Never laid a hand on any woman before."

"I suppose he could have caught her messing around with someone else." Rob played devil's advocate. "Maybe it sent him over the edge. Perhaps he had months of pent-up aggression simmering under the surface and he unleashed it on Bridget when he caught her being unfaithful?"

Jo looked sceptical. "I suppose anything is possible. It's pointless guessing. We'll just have to ask him and see what he says. Although, there was no mention of her cheating on him in the report."

"I agree, it's unlikely, but it could have been kept under wraps. It's possible her parents didn't know or didn't want to admit it."

"But if she was, surely the lover would have come forward?"

Rob shrugged. "No necessarily. Not if he was married."

Jo fell silent. Rob took the M1 turn-off. The traffic was heavy as usual on the motorways around London, but at least it was moving and in the fast lane he managed an impressive seventy miles per hour. According to his satnav, the drive was two and a half hours, which meant they'd get there shortly before noon.

HMP WHITEMOOR WAS a sprawling prison campus amidst acres and acres of agricultural fields and light industrial works. They parked in a purpose-built carpark surrounded by tall trees and freshly-painted white-lines and walked across the tarmac to the entrance. The only way in was through a darkened glass door in the centre of a grey-brick building with a sloping, slate-grey roof and no windows. The only attempt at décor was the Royal prisons insignia mounted above the doorway. The whole place had an air of finality about it.

"Ever been here before," asked Jo, suppressing a shiver.

"Nope. This is a first. You?"

She shook her head.

They went inside and stopped at reception where a petite woman with flaming red hair offset by her cashmere blue jumper sat in front of a computer, her nails clacking away on the keyboard.

Rob thought how out of place she looked. She'd be the type of person you'd expect to see in a smart solicitor's firm or working for a posh finance company.

"Can I help you?" she asked with a smile.

"We're here to see Ron Studley?" Jo held out her warrant card. "I'm Detective Chief Inspector Maguire and this is Detective Inspector Miller."

The woman gazed at their cards for a minute, then nodded. "Please sign in, then you can go through. It's directly across the yard in the grey building."

Was there any other kind of building in this place?

"Someone will take you through security," she added. Once they'd signed in, she pressed a buzzer beneath the desk. There was a loud click and the heavy metal door in front of them released. Rob pushed it open and held it for Jo. She smiled her thanks. "This place gives me the creeps."

"I know what you mean."

He couldn't imagine being incarcerated here and thought about how the inmates must feel when they were brought into the yard for the first time. It was the end of their life as they knew it, with only the grey buildings, the barred windows – he'd yet to see any windows but he imagined the ones that were there would be barred – and the clanging of doors to welcome them.

The concrete yard smelled damp and there were puddles at the sides that hadn't evaporated after the recent rainfall, and probably never would. He glanced up at the overcast sky. Not even the sun saw fit to shine on this place, to help the water dissipate.

Jo stuck close to him as they made their way across the yard and into the next building, also grey brick, also low and sprawling, but with significantly more security than the outer building.

"Put your belongings in here," said a beefy man in a tight-fitting prison uniform holding out a plastic container, much like the ones used at airports. "That includes any electronics and mobile devices."

They did as they were told, then Rob walked through the metal detector, his hands up in front of him. Jo followed suit, after which they were led down a long corridor, through several more automatically controlled security gates, and into a large hall with several tables and chairs. This must be the visiting room.

Rob imagined wives and children greeting imprisoned fathers and felt a sense of sadness descend on him. What was the point? Lives lost, hopes dashed, he could almost sense the desolation in the room.

"Wait here," barked the guard.

Shortly afterwards, a man in a crisp, brown uniform unlike the other guards, opened the door and gestured for them to follow him.

"Your prisoner is waiting in Room Four. It's along the corridor to the left."

They walked ahead of him and stopped outside interview Room 4. The door was locked, but there was a glass panel through which they saw a slender man huddled over the table, his head bowed as if in prayer.

The guard punched in a code and the door swung open.

"I'll be right outside if you need me."

Rob nodded, and they went inside.

RON STUDLEY WASN'T what Rob had expected. He was much thinner, but then six years inside would do that to a man, and his hair that had been dark and full in the police folder was now tinged with grey and thinning. Small veins crisscrossed his temples like a drunken spider's web and disappearing into his hairline and his skin seemed thin, almost translucent. He glanced up as they walked in, his expression a mix of curiosity and resentment.

Rob made the introductions and they sat down. The wooden table between them was bolted to the floor. Rob tried to shuffle forwards and found his chair was too.

He glanced at Jo. In the car they'd decided he'd start off the questioning, just clarifying the basics, then she'd step in and ask the more emotional questions once he'd warmed up. She gave him a little nod.

"Ron – do you mind if I call you Ron?" The prisoner shook his head, which Rob took to be a good sign. He was cooperating. "We'd like to ask you some questions about the night Bridget Kane was murdered."

Ron frowned, but he nodded slowly. So far, his curiosity was overriding his animosity towards the police. "Could you tell us in your own words what happened?"

"I don't know what happened because I wasn't with her that night."

"Okay, could you tell us what you did that night?"

"Sure, I was at home watching football. We'd had a row and Bridget had stormed off. That was the last time I saw her." There was a flicker of sadness in his eyes, but he looked away.

"What was the row about?" Rob asked softly. Jo was observing, a passive, unjudgmental expression on her face.

He shook his head. "It hardly matters now, but we were arguing about whether to have her parents over for dinner. It was her birthday the following week, and I wanted to do something special, just the two of us, but she felt it was time we invited her stuck-up parents over. We'd just moved into a new place, you see, and she wanted to show it off. Show them how well she'd done, and that I was behaving myself."

"I take it you didn't see eye to eye with her parents?" asked Rob.

Ron scoffed. "You could say that."

"What happened after she left?"

"Nothing. I stayed in and watched the game, and then went to bed. The next thing I knew, the coppers were bashing down my door and I was arrested for her murder. I didn't even know she was dead."

"Didn't you worry when she didn't come home that night?" Jo asked in a soft voice, speaking for the first time.

Ron glanced at her. "No, I thought she'd gone to her parents' house. She was in a real huff."

"Did she often go to her parents?"

Ron looked down at the table. "No, not really. We were pretty happy actually, despite what they said about us."

"What did they say?"

"That I had a temper and that we used to row a lot."

"Did you?" Jo was gently probing.

"No, not at all. Bridget understood me. We had a great relationship. We were going to get married, you know? And she was the one who proposed because she said I was taking too long. I couldn't believe she'd want to marry someone like me. I was a mechanic, a grease monkey, and she came from a good family. Her father was some bigwig businessman, he was friends with the mayor and the chief of police, those kinds of people." His voice turned bitter. "I didn't stand a chance."

Jo leaned forward in her chair, her elbows brushing the table. "Did Bridget ever mention anyone following her or watching her in the days leading up to her murder?"

Ron's eyes widened. "Not in the days leading up to her murder, but there was this guy harassing her several months before that. Is that who you mean?"

Rob met Jo's astonished gaze. They'd been right. Their hunch had paid off. Neither of them had really expected it to be that easy. How had the police missed that?

"Could you tell us about that?" asked Jo, who was now clutching the table with both hands.

Ron scrunched up his nose. "She had this ex-boyfriend, some weirdo she'd met at college. I can't remember his name. He'd been calling her and waiting for her outside her work, that sort of thing. He couldn't accept the fact that she'd moved on."

"Did they break up just before you two got together?" Rob asked, wondering if this could be the guy they were after. Was Bridget the girl who'd broken his heart and sent him over the edge? Was she the one who'd set his diabolical killing spree in action?

Ron looked smug. "Actually, they were never really together. It had been a fling, a one-nighter, nothing more, and it meant nothing to Bridget. She met me shortly afterwards and we were pretty hot and heavy for a while, but this guy wouldn't leave her alone. He used to wait for her to finish work then beg her to give him another chance. Pathetic, really. He'd call several times a day until she blocked him from her phone. It got so bad she asked her father to warn him off."

"Did he?" jumped in Jo. "Warn him off?"

"Yes, I think so because she never heard from the guy again." Jo rubbed her forehead. Rob knew she was wondering if they could track down someone who remembered her father warning him off. DCI Becker maybe? Although, the retired policeman hadn't mentioned that.

"How long before she died was that?" Rob wanted to know.

Ron thought for a moment. "It was right after we met, so it would have been at least six months before she died. We moved in together after three months, like I said, we were pretty tight by that stage. It felt natural, you know?"

Rob did know because that's how he'd felt about Yvette. His attraction to her may have been sexual to begin with, but after a few months, when they were still at it like rabbits and it felt so right, he could quite easily have asked her to move in with him. As it was, he'd asked after six months when he'd proposed, and she'd said yes without a second's thought. In retrospect, perhaps she should have taken that second to think about it. Perhaps he should have. He focused on Ron, who had wrapped his arms around himself in a meagre attempt at self-comfort. "And when exactly did you get engaged?"

Rob looked so forlorn that Rob couldn't help but feel sorry for him.

"The week before she died."

16

"Did you give her a ring," Jo asked softly. Rob could tell Jo had come to the same conclusion as he had, that Ron had been set up. He'd been the fall guy in a clever murder plot by Bridget's ex-boyfriend, the man without a name, who had later gone on to become the infamous *Surrey Stalker*.

"No, because I wasn't the one who proposed." His lower lip jutted out like he was trying not to cry. "I was going to get her one, just as soon as my pay check cleared. She said she didn't want anything fancy."

That explained why no ring was mentioned in the report. It hadn't been found on her body or worse, lodged inside her like the others.

"I'm sorry for your loss," murmured Jo, even though it was six years too late. When Ron had been arrested, everyone had assumed he was guilty, and no one would have stopped to think that he was grieving too.

"Does this mean you believe me?" There was hope in the prisoner's voice, hope that Rob wanted to encourage, but knew that he couldn't.

He chose his words carefully. "We're working on a new angle in a current case, and we think this guy, this ex-boyfriend of Bridget's might be involved."

Ron perked up. "Do you think he was the one who murdered Bridget?"

"We don't know yet," cut in Jo, equally conscious about giving the inmate false hope. "It's a line of enquiry in an ongoing investigation. But if you could help us find him, it might give us a better idea of his involvement."

Ron's face fell. "I don't know anything about him. Like I said, I can't even remember his name"

"Are you sure? Bridget must have mentioned it to you at some point," prompted Jo. "Have a think, it might come to you."

Ron shut his eyes, a frown across his brow. He was thinking hard. "He had a high-pitched, nasal voice, I know because I spoke to him once on the phone. Told him to fuck off and leave her alone."

"Did you ever see him?" If they could get a description...

"No, I didn't. He always cornered her when I wasn't around."

"So, he wasn't a local?" asked Rob.

Ron shook his head slowly. "No, I don't think so. Bridget went to college in Canterbury, so maybe he lived there, but I don't know."

"And she never described him?" Jo was clutching at straws. "She didn't mention anything that would help us locate him? The colour of his hair, his eyes, any body piercings or tattoos, that sort of thing?"

Ron closed his eyes again, tapping into long ago memories. "I remember once, after he'd called, she was freaked out and said he was a tall, freaky weirdo." He opened his eyes again. "I don't know if that helps?"

"It does." Jo assured him. "Every little thing helps."

"If you catch this guy, does that mean I can get out of here?"

There was a little light behind Ron's eyes, a light that hadn't been there when they'd walked in.

Jo exhaled. "It's not that simple, I'm afraid. We'd have to link him to Bridget's death, and after all this time..." She faded off, the rest being self-explanatory.

Ron's shoulders slumped. "So even though I'm innocent, I have to rot in here while that psycho is free to do whatever he likes."

Jo leaned forward. "Help us find him, Ron. Try to remember his name. We can only do so much without a name. Once we find him, we can concentrate on linking him to Bridget's death."

Ron beat his forehead with his palm like he was trying to kick-start his brain. "I wish I could, but it was such a long time ago and I haven't given that guy another thought since then. I've had bigger things to worry about."

"I understand." Jo patted his hand. Rob noticed she was a very tactile person, something else he liked about her. She wasn't afraid to reach out and touch people. "If you do remember anything, let us know straight away. You can contact us at the Richmond Police Station. My name is Jo Maguire, and this is Rob Miller."

Even though they'd introduced themselves at the start, Jo reiterated in the hopes that it would sink in. They hadn't been allowed to bring anything in with them, so they had no cards to give him.

Ron nodded, but looked sullen. "I guess it was too much to hope for."

Jo frowned, as if she'd just remembered something. "Ron, do you mind if I ask you how Bridget's clothes got to be in your rubbish bin?"

He sat up straight, immediately on the defensive. "I have no idea. When she left, she was fully clothed."

"I believe hair was found in the boot of your car. Do you know how that got there?"

"No, I don't know how it got into the boot. We'd gone out

earlier in the day to this meadow that we liked to visit. It was our secret spot. We used to make love under the old oak tree in the corner, so her DNA would have been all over my car, but as far as I know, she never got into the boot."

"Meadow? Which meadow was that?" Rob felt a twinge of anticipation. The grass stains.

Ron arched his eyebrows, surprised by the question. "It's just before Barham on the Valley Road, off the A2. Why is that important?"

"There were grass stains on the back of Bridget's jacket and on her heels, suggesting she was dragged across a field or a meadow," Jo explained. "The prosecution thought that's where she was killed."

"I thought she was found on the beach?" Ron seemed confused. It was clear he hadn't paid much attention at the trial, which wasn't surprising considering he would have been devastated by Bridget's death and bewildered by the sudden turn of events. "Wasn't she killed there?"

"Could the grass stains have been from earlier in the day, from the meadow?" Rob stared at him intently, ignoring his previous question. This was important.

"Yes, I suppose so." He smiled sadly. "We made out under the oak tree on the grass. It was a spur of the moment thing. We were driving by and hadn't been there for a while, so we thought it would be fun..."

Would that account for the grass stains on her jacket and heels? Vigorous sex, yes, certainly.

Rob exhaled. "Okay, thanks Ron. You've been extremely helpful."

"Really?" He couldn't see how the meadow related to the case at all.

Jo smiled and stood up. "Please have a think about that name and get hold of me. Richmond Police Station."

He nodded.

They left the room, a sense of excitement surrounded them. Rob couldn't wait to get back to the car and discuss what they'd found out. He glanced through the glass pane as the door shut and saw Ron staring into the corner of the room, a faraway look in his eyes, lost in the past.

17

—————

By the time they got back from the prison, Jo and Rob had discussed every angle of the Bridget Kane case and settled on a plan of action. First, they needed to request the call records from Bridget's phone going back six months before she died. If her ex-boyfriend had been harassing her, then his number would show up on the records.

"That might be enough to ID him," Jo said hopefully.

Rob thought it more likely a guy like the stalker would use a prepaid burner phone, so there'd be no trace, but he didn't want to spoil the mood. It was worth checking, for sure. Back then... his first victim... he may not have been so smart.

Secondly, they needed to speak to Bridget's mother. Jo called retired chief Becker from the car and learned the mother was still alive and living in semi-sheltered housing on the outskirts of Deal. According to the retired detective, her mental faculties were still intact, so she might just remember her husband going after Bridget's ex to warn him off. Becker himself had no recollection of the incident, and it certainly hadn't been reported to the police.

On the way to Deal the next morning, they planned to stop at the meadow Ron had talked about to see if they could find the oak tree. Unfortunately, Bridget had long since been buried, so unless they exhumed the body, they wouldn't be able to match the grass on her heels with any samples they collected.

"If she did get the stains from earlier in the day, we can rule out her being murdered there," pointed out Rob.

"So, she could, in fact, have been killed at the beach?" Jo said. "But given the fact that it would still have been light at seven the previous evening, surely someone would have seen them or heard her screaming? You can't rape and strangle someone on an exposed public beach at sunset without someone noticing."

"Which means he killed her somewhere else and dumped her body on the beach during the night."

"Well, at least that explains why he didn't leave her in the field."

Rob turned to glance at her. "Yes, but it still leaves us without a primary crime scene."

"We'll probably never know," said Jo woefully. "But if we can trace this guy, we might be able to pin Julie and Sara's murders on him."

They could dare to dream.

ROB'S PHONE rang as they walked into the squad room. It was Mallory. His deputy hung up as soon as he saw them. "I'm glad you're back. Gowan, the pathologist, just called. He's got something on that duct-tape."

Jo's face lit up. "DNA evidence?"

"Yeah, a small amount. He's sent it to the lab. Maybe we'll get a hit on this one."

"That's great news." Rob thumped him on the back.

Please let it turn up something.

"If the guy's got a record, we'll have him." Mallory grinned. "Things are looking up. How'd it go at Whitemoor?"

Rob filled him in while Jo went to brief Lawrence. She flashed him a smile as she headed to the boss's office. "Great work today, partner."

"You too," he called after her.

"You two seem to be getting along well," Mallory remarked, giving Rob a knowing look. Rob ignored it and told Mallory their theory about Ron Studley.

"Poor guy," muttered Mallory when he was finished. "Imagine spending six years in that shit-hole for a crime you didn't commit."

"Yeah, on top of losing your loved one." Rob shook his head. "The worst thing is, even if we catch this guy, it's unlikely we'll be able to link him to Bridget Kane's murder, which means Ron won't get his get out of jail free card."

"The stalker could confess," said Mallory. "You never know, these serial killers want people to know what they did, they like the attention. It feeds their ego."

At Rob's surprised look, he added, "I read the profile on the stalker, it's all in there."

Rob hadn't had the time, so he just nodded. "Let me know when you find a match on that fingerprint."

He called Gowan to thank him. "Don't get too excited, it's only a partial. It was on the tape covering her mouth."

"We're running it now," said Rob, unable to keep the hopefulness out of his voice. "So, there was nothing else? No DNA inside of her or under her fingernails?"

"No, I'm afraid not. I can tell you the brand of condom he wore, if you want? We were able to identify it from the residue. It's a common brand, available at any pharmacy."

"That doesn't help much," admitted Rob. It might if they had an inkling as to where this guy lived, but they couldn't very well go into every pharmacy in the county asking if they remembered a tall guy in a hoodie buying condoms. Chances were he didn't wear the hoodie when he wasn't out stalking, and without it, they wouldn't be able to identify him.

"How about that drink?" Jo asked Rob when she returned from Lawrence's office. She'd been in there a while, updating him on their afternoon and the next steps they'd proposed. Her cheeks were flushed and her eyes shone with excitement - they were getting somewhere. Finally.

Rob thought about his cold, empty house.

"Why not?" There didn't seem any point in going home, besides, he wanted to go over that report the profiler had put together. He said as much to Jo, who nodded towards her brief-case. "I've got it with me. We can dissect it over a beer."

That did sound good.

They left the police station and walked up the High Street. It was well lit with the popular local restaurants doing a lively trade.

"How about down here?" Rob gestured to a narrow alleyway which wound down towards Richmond Green. Jo was from up north originally, now based in central London, so she didn't know the area. "There's a great pub on the right. It's quiet and has good food in case we fancy a bite."

"Perfect." She smiled and followed him down the alley lit by old-fashioned Victorian lamps that cast a coppery glow onto the cobblestones. *The Britannia*, a quaint Victorian pub, was sand-wiched between two other similar buildings and was the type of place you wouldn't notice unless you knew it was there. It was an eighteenth-century brick building with a parapet, two windows wide and three storeys high. The yellow gleam emanating through the sash windows was cosy and inviting.

"It's so quaint," breathed Jo as she pushed open the door and they went inside. The interior was surprisingly large and covered the entire ground floor.

Rob led her to a table at the back where they'd have a modicum of privacy. They passed a well-stocked fire that crackled reassuringly and threw a rosy glimmer onto the dark-wood tables. There were a few television screens mounted to the walls showing golfing highlights. Rob remembered that in the real world, the one where people went about their normal lives, the Masters was on.

As Jo took off her jacket, she twisted her body towards him, and he caught himself staring at the V in her neckline. He averted his gaze before she noticed.

They sat beside each other rather than opposite, so they could both view the report. He was suddenly very aware of her closeness. A waitress came over and took their order.

"Do you come here often?" Jo asked, while they waited for their drinks.

"Occasionally, when I need the peace and quiet in which to think. Otherwise, I go to *The Cricketer* which is just around the corner, but that's rowdier and more suited to after-work drinks than to reviewing case files."

She chuckled and reached down to get the folder in question out of her briefcase. Her blouse escaped from the band of her skirt and he glimpsed a flash of pale skin. The waitress returned with two pints of lager and a bowl of crisps which she set down between them.

Jo opened the folder while Rob took a long draw on his beer. God, he needed this. It felt great going down his throat and he resisted the urge to go 'aah' at the end of it.

"The profile is pretty detailed," she said. "The forensic psychologist asked a lot of questions and I told him what I knew about our suspect and the crime scenes, mainly from reading your and Mallory's reports."

Rob nodded and read the introduction. "White male, late

twenties to early thirties, tall in stature. This is all stuff we already know."

"Yes, I gave him that much. He builds on it from there."

"Emotionally unstable childhood probably consisting of inappropriate interests or obsessions. Prone to bouts of violence and temper tantrums." He glanced up. "We don't know any of this for sure, only that he lost it after his girlfriend dumped him."

"And according to Ron, she wasn't really his girlfriend, just a one-night-stand, which means he has an irrational and unrealistic view of relationships." She pointed to a paragraph where the profiler had said just that.

Rob read on. "Our suspect probably had a dysfunctional family life with divorced or separated parents, frequent arguments resulting in a messy break-up." He gave a wry grin. "That could be said for a lot of people. They don't all turn out to be serial killers."

Jo snorted in response.

Rob carried on. "He was probably an introvert at school, unpopular or bullied, certainly socially awkward." He glanced up. "Well, that makes sense given how he reacted to his fling with Bridget. For him it was a big deal, perhaps his first love affair. For her, it was a drunken night out, a mistake."

Jo's hand was wrapped around her beer glass, even though she'd yet to have a sip. "We know that Bridget dumping him was the catalyst. It spurred him on to commit murder for the first time."

"But only when she got engaged to Ron." Rob pointed out. "That seemed to be the trigger. He harassed her after the break-up, but he only killed her when she got engaged."

"How did he know?" asked Jo suddenly. "How did he know she was engaged?"

"He must have been watching her all that time." Rob frowned. "Ron and Bridget had been together six months before she proposed to him. That's a long time to stalk somebody, to remain in the shadows."

Jo shuddered. "Talk about obsessive."

She did take a drink after that, a big one, downing at least a quarter of the pint, as if she was trying to banish the creepy thoughts in her head.

"Hey, go easy," he said when she gave a little splutter.

She grinned. "I tend to be a bit extreme. Nothing in half measures."

He gazed at her wet lips and twinkling blue eyes. "Does that extend to your work too?"

She shrugged. "I guess so. I work long hours, like we all do, which is why I don't have a social life." She gazed into her glass. "It's a bit sad, really."

"I understand. I don't socialise other than work drinks with the team after we close a case, or perhaps the odd one after work, like this."

She gave a half-smile. "I'm glad to know I'm not the only one."

He studied her for a long moment, then against his better judgment, said, "So I guess you're not seeing anyone?"

"You guessed right." She met his gaze and he felt a flutter in the vicinity of his lower abdomen, but then she glanced down at the table. "I don't have the time to dedicate to anyone else. When I'm on a case it takes up every waking moment of my life. When I'm not at work, I'm thinking about it, and when I am at work, I keep going until I can't keep my eyes open any longer."

Those words could have come straight out of his own mouth.

"I know exactly what you mean," he said dryly.

"How about you?" She turned to him. "Are you seeing anyone?"

He knew what he should say, but the truth was, he wasn't sure about anything. He pictured Yvette's face at the cocktail bar.

I'm not sure you're what I want anymore.

Instead, he shook his head. "My girlfriend moved out a couple of days ago, thanks to the hours I was putting in on this case, and now I have no idea where we stand."

"I'm sorry to hear that." Jo tugged the elastic band out of her hair. It was much longer than he expected and fell in a wavy blonde cascade down her back. "Do you think she'll come back?"

"I don't know," he said honestly. He wanted her to come back, or at least he thought he did, but then he gazed at Jo's hair falling over her shoulder, the hollow at the base of her neck, and the soft blush on her cheeks and he wasn't so sure.

"It's an occupational hazard," she said softly. "No one understands what it's like, unless they're in the game themselves."

How true that was. Perhaps he was crazy trying to make it work with Yvette. It was so obvious she didn't understand, nor even attempted to understand the type of work he did. She had no idea of the pressure he was under, or the deep-seated desire that drove him to pursue dangerous criminals and get them off the streets.

But Jo did. She lived and breathed it every day like he did. To her it wasn't just a job, it was a vocation. Same as most of his team. They were in first thing in the morning, often pulling all-nighters, or spending hours on mundane jobs like scrolling through CCTV footage or going door-to-door looking for anyone who might or might not have seen something.

"What else is in the report," he said, feeling the heat from her thigh seeping into his. Somehow, she'd moved closer to him, almost shoulder to shoulder. He reached for his beer.

"It says he's likely to have some sort of disability that he's ashamed of." Her hair fell forward onto the document and he brushed it aside. It was soft to the touch. She didn't react, nor did she move away.

"That's a peculiar thing to say." He tried to focus on the material in front of him instead of her. "How did he come to that conclusion?"

She frowned slightly as she tried to remember. "I hope I get this right, but it was a deduction based on the crimes he'd already committed. The secluded locations where he wasn't likely to come into contact with anyone else, the fact that none of his victims had been approached in a crowd or manipulated into going along with him, and that he surprised them all in the middle of nowhere. This means our killer felt awkward or ashamed about himself. Overpowering an unsuspecting victim and being able to dominate and control her was his way of overcoming this handicap."

Rob nodded slowly. It made sense. "Well, I don't think it's a physical disability, based on his physique and the nature of the crimes. He'd need a certain degree of strength to overcome his victims, particularly since we know they put up a fight. And he'd need both hands to strangle them, or to hold them down while he assaulted them."

"Indeed." Jo reached for her glass and downed the rest of her lager. It seemed she was incapable of taking just one sip. All or nothing.

"So, are we talking about a stutter here, or a lisp, or maybe even a limp?"

"Or possibly bad acne scarring, or some other skin condition. Bad teeth, even."

Rob rubbed the stubble on his chin. "It didn't look like it from the partial profile shot, but then he did have some facial hair which would cover any scarring."

"Perhaps Bridget's mother will be able to shed some light tomorrow?"

He leaned back in his chair. "Let's hope so."

"DO YOU LIVE LOCALLY?" Jo asked, as they strolled back down the

High Street towards the station. Even though they had an early start the next day, neither was rushing to get home.

"Yeah, I'm off Kew Road, the other side of Richmond Circus." He grinned. "It takes me a whole ten minutes to get to work in the mornings, which is why I chose it. How about you?"

He knew she lived in central London.

"I'm in Borough," she said with a little shake of her head. "It's a great area, close to the market and really vibey, which I like, but it's a good ten-minute walk from Waterloo station."

Rob knew his next words would condemn him.

"You're welcome to stay at mine tonight. I've got the whole house to myself, and the couch is moderately comfortable." He rolled his eyes. "I can vouch for that."

It seemed he'd slept there more often than not recently.

She laughed. "Are you sure you don't mind? It would be easier than going all the way home, just to come back at the crack of dawn tomorrow."

"No, of course not. Come on, it's this way."

He led her across the busy roundabout at the bottom of the High Street and down Kew Road which was just as busy with people spilling out of bars and restaurants and making their way towards the station. He was aware of her heels clicking on the pavement beside him and her arm brushing against his every so often.

She waited while he opened the door. The floorboards creaked as they stepped into the dark hallway. He fumbled for the lights.

"Sorry about the mess." He gathered the scatter cushions up off the floor and picked up an old coffee mug he'd left on the table beside the couch. Apart from that, it wasn't in too bad a shape, thank God. He hadn't cleaned since Yvette had left, partly because he'd been so busy but also because of the listlessness that he'd felt at the state of his relationship.

He wasn't feeling listless now.

"Can I get you a drink? I've got beer and I think there's some Prosecco left in the fridge."

"I'll have a beer, thanks." She put her briefcase down and followed him to the kitchen. "Do you have anything to eat? I'm starving."

"I wouldn't hold your breath." Rob opened the fridge and looked around. There was a loaf of bread, some cheese and a few tomatoes. "How about a sandwich?"

"Great, I'll make it," she said, reaching over him to grab the items off the shelf. He caught a faint smell of vanilla as she brushed past him.

Without really thinking what he was doing, he slipped an arm around her waist. She turned towards him and paused, her gaze lifted until it met his. Slowly, he drew her towards him. She allowed it to happen and closed the fridge door behind her before wrapping her arms around his neck. She wanted this too.

He bent his head and kissed her, holding her close against his chest. She felt soft and fragrant and he breathed her in, losing himself in the moment. He felt her sigh as she closed her eyes and kissed him back.

18

It took Rob a moment to realise it wasn't Yvette lying next to him when he woke up the next morning. Instead of dark hair spread out against the pillow, it was blonde, and while Yvette had olive skin and a sculptured bone structure, Jo was pale and soft, her features more rounded and sensual. He lay quietly comparing the two women, wondering what had made him act so rashly last night. Jo was great, there was no doubt about it, and they had this connection that was hard to ignore, but he was engaged. Sure, they were having problems, but that didn't mean he had to run off and sleep with the first available woman that came along.

He frowned as the guilt descended.

Not to mention the fact that Jo was his superior, as well as being part of the murder squad. They really shouldn't have done this. Lawrence would have a shit-fit if he found out.

"Having regrets already?" she asked, rolling onto her side, her mouth curved into a sardonic smile.

He grimaced. "Am I that easy to read?"

She shrugged and sat up, not bothering to cover her breasts.

"It's written all over your face, but you don't have to worry. I'm not going to say anything. Nobody need find out about this."

He nodded, unsure of himself. His confusion prevented him from responding. She saved him from having to by throwing back the covers and getting up. "Do you mind if I take a shower?"

"Of course not. Go ahead. I'll rustle up something for breakfast."

"Thanks, I'm ravenous. We never did get around to making that sandwich." She threw him a mischievous look and he grinned, despite himself. Last night had been amazing, and despite his guilt, it had felt good to be wanted, to be loved. Jo had been a thoughtful lover, giving and taking in equal measure, and while it didn't have the urgency or the heat of Yvette's frantic love-making, it seemed deeper somehow, and more substantial. That's what worried him.

When she came downstairs smelling of shampoo twenty minutes later, she was in the same clothes as yesterday. Her hair hung sleek and damp down her back, and her face was freshly scrubbed and devoid of make-up. That was something else he wasn't used to. Yvette always applied her make-up as soon as she'd bathed in the morning. He had to admit, Jo looked fantastic.

He touched her arm. "I'm sorry if I acted like a jerk. I think I surprised myself by what happened last night and I'm not sure how I feel about it yet. My girlfriend has only just left."

She put a hand on his cheek. "I get it, don't worry. It was fun, don't get me wrong, but I'm not looking for a relationship. This won't affect our working relationship."

How could it not? But he didn't argue the point. He was just relieved there was no awkwardness between them. "I made toasted cheese sandwiches." He pointed to the table where he'd placed several of them. "And the coffee's nearly ready."

"Bliss." She sat down and tucked into one of the toasties. He watched for any sign of stiffness or feminine pique, like Yvette was so fond of using, but there was none. She really did seem fine with it. So, he sat down opposite her. "You know, you're so easy to be with," he said, reaching for the plate. "I was expecting this to be awkward as hell."

"No need," she said, her mouth full. "We both wanted it, and we're both content to leave it at that. Am I right?"

He nodded.

"So, what's the problem? Can I have some of that coffee? I'm gasping."

"Sure." He took the filter jug out of the machine and poured them each a cup, then he leaned back and watched her as she took a sip. On her face was an expression of pure joy. "Okay, you get ten out of ten for the coffee. After this, I don't know how you can drink that shit at the station."

"Needs be..." He chuckled and took a bite of his sandwich. "How do you feel about heading straight off to Kent this morning? I'd like to talk to Bridget's mother as soon as possible."

Her blue eyes met his across the table. "We'll have to go into the office first, else they'll know something is up. It's bad enough I'm wearing the same clothes as yesterday." She grimaced at her crumpled blouse and he had visions of last night when he'd hastily unbuttoned it and peeled it off her.

"You could always borrow one of Yvette's," he blurted out, then instantly regretted it. Of course, she wouldn't want to wear his girl-friend's clothes.

To his surprise, she nodded. "Actually, if you wouldn't mind, that would be great. It would save face, too."

"I'll see if I can find you something." He went upstairs and had a quick rummage through Yvette's wardrobe. She'd taken a lot of stuff, more than he'd realised, which made him wonder if she had any intention of coming back. Finally, he settled on a navy-blue silk blouse that he thought would do. It was smart enough for work but not too dressy.

"How's this?" He returned to the kitchen and held it up for her to see.

"Perfect." She took it from him and disappeared into the lounge. She was back in less than two minutes, tucking the blouse into her skirt. It looked fantastic with her blonde hair which was drying and floated in wispy strands around her face.

It also made him think of Yvette, and a fresh wave of guilt washed over him. No, maybe not guilt – confusion.

"I think I'll get going now." She stuffed her old blouse into her briefcase which she'd brought with her from the living room. "It's probably best if we don't show up together."

He walked her to the front door and there was an awkward moment, the only one of the morning, where he felt like he ought to kiss her or hug her or something, but she took the decision away from him.

"I'll see you in a bit," she said, not meeting his eye, and without waiting for a reply, she turned and marched smartly up the street. In Yvette's blouse. Her blonde hair flowing out behind her.

Jo's team had requisitioned the phone records and it was these she had on her lap as Rob drove the hundred-and-fourteen miles to Deal on the Kentish coast.

"Six months before Bridget Kane died would make it August 2011." Jo's yellow highlighter poised above the print-outs.

"Yeah. Ron Studley told us he called her almost daily, sometimes more than once a day and that was just after they'd got together."

"I'll have to rule out these other numbers first. She flicked through the pages. "Her parents, for instance, and her work. Not to mention Ron, himself."

"They should be in the original case file." Rob kept his eyes on the road. The M25 traffic was still heavy, it being the tail-end of the morning rush-hour. It was a chilly, overcast day, with temperatures below average for this time of year. The thermometer on his dashboard read six degrees Celsius.

"Ah, got it." She fished in her briefcase for a pen and scribbled a couple of numbers down on a notepad before picking up the highlighter and going back to the phone records.

Rob let her concentrate, and before long he heard her running the highlighter over a couple of rows.

"Found it?" He glimpsed at the document on her lap.

"Yeah, I think so. There's one number here that's incoming and frequent, like every day and the calls never last longer than a minute."

"Sounds promising."

"It's an 075 number, so probably O2, but whether it's a contract or pre-paid phone, I can't tell."

"Ask Mallory to follow that up." Rob was putting money on a burner phone. The stalker wouldn't have risked using his own, but then again, he may not have realised he was going to kill Bridget at that stage.

"That's okay, I'll put Gary on it."

Rob turned off the M25 onto the M26 and then a short time later onto the M20 towards Dover. The landscape opened up as the Surrey Hills flashed by, luscious and languid on either side of the motorway. Jo didn't glance up, she was riveted by the call records.

"Then the calls suddenly stop," she announced. "Around late November he ceases to call altogether. It's a very sudden turn-around, don't you think?"

"He obviously realised he wasn't getting anywhere."

"Maybe that's when she moved in with Ron. He did say it was about three months after they met, didn't he?"

"Yes, that's right. So, he gives up calling and takes up stalking instead."

Jo glanced sideways at him. "And he stalks her in secret for another three months before he finally decides to kill her." She shook her head.

"Triggered by their engagement," added Rob.

Jo got on the phone and called her deputy, Gary Steward, who said he would trace the phone number, if it could be traced.

"It's starting to come together." Jo stashed the folder in her briefcase at her feet. "It makes sense: the timing of the phone calls, what Ron said, and how the stalker finally lost it and murdered her."

Rob sharing her excitement, put his foot down on the accelerator, eager to get to Deal to find out what Bridget's mother had to say. The car surged forward obligingly. "And once he'd killed her, he realised he could get away with it, and so he carried on doing it. It made him feel empowered."

"I wonder how many other women's lives he's destroyed that we don't know about?" Her voice was low. "Six years is a long time. I'll bet there's more out there."

"We did look at as many cold cases as we could," Rob said. "None of them matched his M.O."

"Maybe, I'll put my team on it as well," she mused turning her head to gaze out of the window. "Six years..."

Rob had to agree. The likelihood of Julie being his first victim since Bridget was slim. He didn't mind sharing resources, in fact, having the extra manpower was a blessing since his team was bogged down with the CCTV footage and trawling the feedback from the expo companies, neither of which had turned up anything useful in the last few days.

Jo took out her phone and punched off some text messages, and they drove on in a companionable silence until they got to Dover, where Rob suggested they stop for a coffee. Not wanting to waste any time, they got take-aways and climbed back into the car to search for the meadow that Ron had told them about.

They drove through Lydden and Shepherdswell before they saw a signpost for Barham. "There!" Jo pointed to the left. Rob indicated and turned into a narrow arterial road flanked on either side by golden rape fields. After about a mile, the fields on the right-hand side were replaced by tall trees and a low hedge, which ran parallel to the road.

"Hang on a minute." Jo leaned forward and peered across Rob's chest at a gap in the hedge. Once again, he got a whiff of her freshly washed hair. Her scent was becoming familiar to him. "I think I saw a meadow through there."

He pulled over and they walked back towards the opening. A wooden bridge covered a murky ditch filled with run-off but on the other side, beyond the tree line was a picturesque little meadow and in the far corner an enormous ancient oak.

"This must be it." Rob strode ahead into the meadow. It was a pretty place completely secluded from the road and on the opposite side, the houses that were set much further back behind another row of trees. "I can see why they came here."

"It would be beautiful in summer." Jo pulled her jacket tighter around her. The cold was seeping through making her shiver.

"Do you want to take a sample?" Rob gazed up at the big old oak. He wondered how many stories it had to tell.

"I will, although I don't think it'll do any good." Jo took a small plastic bag out of her jacket pocket. She bent down beneath the oak tree and plucked some samples of the grass. "If Bridget hadn't been buried we could have compared them to the grazes on her heels."

"Who did the post-mortem?" Rob asked suddenly. "They might have done an analysis already, in which case we just need to compare the two."

Jo's face lit up. "You're right. Now why didn't I think of that?" She winked at him and a warm glow spread throughout his body.

"Lack of sleep must be clouding my brain. I'll check the file when we get back to the car."

Mrs. Kane lived in a small residential block of flats two roads back from the beachfront. It was identical to the buildings on either side, red brick, two-stories high with sea-weathered white doors and window frames.

"Fernwood House," read Jo as they came to a stop. "That's the place."

"She's flat number seven." Rob got out of the car and pulled on his jacket. Down here by the seaside the wind felt even more bitter.

They rang number seven's buzzer from downstairs and a robotic female voice asked them to please wait. A few moments later, it told them the door was now unlocked and to please enter.

Jo pushed open the front door and they went inside. Flat seven was up the stairs to the right. "After you," said Rob, standing back to let her go first. The stairs were only wide enough for one person at a time. They heard a door open and by the time they reached the top, a short woman with shoulder-length hair that had almost completely faded to white, stood waiting for them.

"You must be the detectives," she said with a thin smile. "Please come in."

They followed her into her apartment. It was bigger than Rob had expected, with large windows that let in plenty of light, and carpeting that looked and smelled new.

Jo held out her hand. "I'm DCI Jo Maguire and this is DI Rob Miller. Thanks so much for seeing us."

She gestured for them to sit. "I don't get much company these days. It's nice to have visitors. Shall I make us some tea?"

Even though they'd had coffee not long before, Rob didn't like to be disagreeable, so he nodded.

"That would be lovely," Jo said in agreement.

Mrs. Kane was painstakingly slow, and it was a good ten minutes later before she brought out a tray laden with cups, saucers and a plate full of biscuits.

"Here, let me pour," said Jo jumping up. Rob could sense her impatience. He too, was desperate to hear what she had to say about her daughter's mysterious stalker.

"Er, Mrs. Kane, do you mind if I jump in and ask you some questions about Bridget?"

She straightened up and looked at him like she'd forgotten this wasn't a social call. "Oh, yes. Of course, dear. Let me sit down."

"Here you go." Jo handed her a cup of tea with a biscuit. The old lady took it gratefully. "Thank you, dear." Then she turned her attention to Rob, who had perched at the end of a cavernous armchair that looked like it might swallow him whole if he sat too far back in it. "What did you want to know?"

"Before Bridget met Ron Studley, she had been seeing a man she met at Canterbury College. I don't know if you can remember, but he gave her quite a hard time when she started dating Ron. He called her incessantly, wouldn't leave her alone."

Mrs. Kane stared at him for a long moment, her pale blue eyes unwavering. He thought perhaps she hadn't grasped what he was saying, and opened his mouth to repeat the question, when she said quietly, "I do remember him. My husband had to have a word to make him leave her alone."

"Yes." Jo almost dropped her biscuit into her tea. "That's the man. You wouldn't by any chance remember his name?"

The old lady crinkled up her forehead, her bushy eyebrows almost completely covering her eyes. Rob found he was holding his breath.

After an excruciating minute, she exhaled.

Jo raised her eyebrows expectantly. "Yes?"

"I think his name was Russel."

19

T hings moved pretty quickly after that. Mrs. Kane couldn't remember Russel's surname, but that didn't matter too much, at least they had a starting point. The old lady was pretty confident about his first name, saying she'd had an uncle called Russel who'd been in the parachute regiment, which is why she remembered, although unfortunately, Bridget's Russel had turned out to be rather a disappointment.

She had no idea how much so.

After confirming which college Bridget had attended, Jo placed a call to her deputy. "Ron, I need you to get hold of Canterbury College and look at the attendance records for the years 2010 and 2011. See if anyone with the first name Russel pops up."

Rob drove as fast as he dared back to Richmond. He even put the siren on and flashed his lights repeatedly to warn motorists to get out the way. Like the Red Sea, the passing-lane opened up before him and they raced along the M20 and then the M25 without any issues. Jo spent the better part of the two-hour journey on the phone.

"We've got six possibilities," she told Rob, holding the phone away from her ear. "Gary has requested the student files and has contacted the DVLA to see if we can get photographs from their driver's licenses."

When Ron, who'd relocated back to Scotland Yard for access to the phone records, managed to get hold of the information, Rob's team were packed into the incident room, awaiting a hastily-called briefing. There was dead silence as Jo's phone rang.

Her voice rang out in the silence. "Yes. Great. Can you send them through to my phone, and copy in DI Miller? Yes, now. Thanks."

She hung up. "The driver's license photographs are coming through now."

Rob got to it. "Listen up, guys. A lot has happened in a very short space of time." He filled them in on the possibility of another suspect in Bridget Kane's murder, someone she'd met at college who'd become obsessed with her and harassed her for some time afterwards.

"We know his first name is Russel, and Jo contacted Canterbury College to see what more they can give us." He gestured for Jo to take over.

"They've come back with six students who have Russel as their first name. I'm waiting for the DVLA to send through photographs on all of them."

On cue, her phone beeped several times in a row. "That will be them now."

Rob felt his phone vibrate simultaneously in his pocket.

"We'll reconvene once we've had a chance to look at these," she told them. No one moved. They all waited for Rob and Jo to glance at their phones.

Rob looked at the first photograph. The man was short – too short – with a full head of brown hair and a pug-nosed face. His name was Russel Bromley. Rob scrolled to the next photograph. Taller, but Asian. Not him either.

The next photo was of a well-developed black guy with shoulders a wrestler would be proud of. Rob scrolled on. Three left to go.

Russel Makings was next, a blond-haired man with pale, pock-marked skin. He showed it to Jo, who was also on the same one. "What do you think?"

"Hmm... maybe? I don't know. He has the bad skin but is it bad enough for him to have developed a social conscious about it? He looks okay to me."

"Yeah, I'm not sold either."

Jo flicked to the next photograph, this time the guy had a turban. Definitely not him.

Last one.

Rob stood by Jo's side, the rest of the room looking on as she brought up the photograph. The name was Russel Hargreaves. He gazed at it, blinked, then looked at it again.

"I know this guy," he said.

"What? How?" Jo demanded, turning to face him.

Rob felt the colour drain from his face. "He was with Yvette at the cocktail bar the other night. I thought he was gay."

"Are you sure? It could be a different guy?"

Rob studied the picture again. Tall, slim, bald head, angular features, everything except the beard. "It's definitely him. He works at Harrods and his name is Simon, I think. Not Russel."

"He could easily have changed his name." Her blue eyes were creased with concern. "Harrods, you say?"

Rob nodded. He felt weak. What did this mean? Was the stalker friends with Yvette? Had he somehow realised who Yvette was engaged to and was now homing in on her?

"Jesus," He looked around in horror. "He's going after her."

"Who? Yvette?" Jo grabbed him by the arm. "How do you know? Rob, what's going on?"

"Don't you see?" He ran a shaky hand through his hair. "He

knows who I am. He's seen me on the news and he knows I'm hunting him. He also knows that Yvette and I are engaged. As my fiancé, she's the perfect target."

"Engaged?" Jo shook her head, trying to understand. "You're engaged?"

He shook his head. "We were, before she walked out. I don't know what we are now. But the point is, *he* doesn't know that."

DCI Lawrence, who'd been listening at the back, surged forward and swung into action. "Okay, we need to get hold of her now. Rob, where is she? Where is she right this minute?"

"Er..." Rob found he was shaking. "She'll be at work, most likely. Harrods, the cosmetics department."

"Okay, let's send uniform down there to pick her up, as well as this Simon character." He glanced at Jo. "Now."

She nodded and issued the command into her phone.

Rob was already scrolling for Yvette's number, but he pushed the wrong button his hands were shaking so badly.

"She'll be okay, Rob, it's just gone four o'clock. He won't risk taking her in the middle of the afternoon in a busy store like Harrods." Lawrence put a big hand on his shoulder.

"She's not answering. I'd better get down there."

Lawrence nodded.

"Jo, stay on the line with the officers picking her up. I want to know when she's safe. That's a priority."

"Will do."

Rob fled from the room with only one thought in his head: To get to Yvette before the stalker did. He could have secured the job at Harrods in order to get close to her, to learn her routine. Christ, why didn't he put two and two together earlier? Yvette would still be wearing her engagement ring, hell, she'd probably told him all about their relationship, his job, the case he was working on.

Fuck. Could it get any worse?

As he drove like a madman towards Harrods, Rob called

Yvette's sister. "Naomi, did Yvette leave for work as usual this morning?"

"Yes, why is something wrong?" The concern was evident in her tone.

"I'm not sure yet. I'll let you know." He hung up and put his foot down, screeching around corners, the siren screaming. Half an hour later he pulled up in front of Harrods in a loading bay. He left the car door open and charged inside, flashing his warrant card to the surprised security guards who immediately followed him through the plush halls and into the cosmetics department. There, he found two uniformed police officers talking to Yvette's supervisor, Rose. He ran up to her and gripped her by the shoulders. "Rose, where's Yvette?"

She had a confused expression on her face. "Why, I was just telling these officers that she went on her tea break forty-five minutes ago and hasn't come back. I was just about to ring her. It's not like her to be late."

Rob's heart sank.

Please let them not be too late.

He turned to the coppers. "Have you got hold of Simon yet?"

"No, we don't know his last name. One of our men is with human resources now."

Rob groaned in irritation. He turned back to Rose. "Who's her friend, the gay guy, Simon someone? He works here too."

"You mean Simon Burridge?" a young woman standing nearby asked. She wore a long black pencil skirt and a white blouse, the standard attire for the sales assistants at Harrods. "He works on the fourth floor in the Bridal Boutique."

"Bridal Boutique?"

That was how he was finding the girls, not the expo at Olympia. Harrods would have a mailing list and he was willing to bet both Julie Andrews and Sara Bakshi were on it. "Which way?" he snapped.

The woman pointed to an elaborate archway through which Rob caught a glimpse of an elevator. "Come with me," he said to the officers and dashed off. They stayed on his heels, as did the security guards, as he sprinted up three flights of escalators, taking two at a time, to the fourth floor.

"Where's the wedding department?" he rasped, chest heaving. The two police officers were panting too, but the fit security guards didn't appear to be out of breath.

"That way," one of them said in a deep, Slavic accent, and headed off through the store, zigzagging around customers, from one luxuriously decorated room to the next.

Eventually, they came to a white room filled with designer wedding gowns and accessories. The Bridal Boutique. Rob ran up to the sales assistant and asked for Simon Burridge. The woman seemed startled. "I-I don't know. I've been calling him for the last hour. He went on his tea break and didn't come back."

God no. He was too late.

Rob gripped the front desk for support and tried to get his breath back. What now? He couldn't think, his mind was clouded with panic. He pulled out his phone and called Jo. He needed her calm, logical, one-step-ahead brain. "He's already got her. Oh, God, Jo. We're too late."

He began to pace up and down the panic heaving in his chest. The police officers and the security guards gave him a wide berth. They didn't know the details, but they could sense this was big.

"Rob, calm down and think." Jo's voice was steady, but he could hear the urgency in her tone. "What's Yvette's mobile number? Is her phone on?"

He thought for a moment. "Yes, it was on, but she didn't pick up."

"Give it to me."

He did and heard her writing it down. "What about this

Simon? Does he have a mobile number that we can trace? Ask them."

Thank God for Jo. His brain wasn't functioning properly due to the shock. He turned back to the sales assistant. "You said you'd been trying to call him. What's his number?"

She read it out to him and he repeated it to Jo at the other end of the line.

"Okay, I've got it," she said. "We're running a trace on both of their phones now. I'll let you know when we get something. Stay on the line."

"Will do." Rob was sick to the stomach at the thought of Yvette at the hands of that monster. God only knew how he got her out of the building.

"Christ, we have to find him Jo. I couldn't bear it if anything happened to..."

"That's not going to happen," she interjected, cutting him off. "We're going to find her. Hang in there. Don't fall apart on me now."

She was right. He had to get a grip. He needed to be functioning optimally if he was going to find this bastard. Adrenalin surged through his veins, replacing the shock.

"Give me something to go on," he whispered. "Anything."

"I'm working on it," she replied. "Mallory's on the line with the tech guys now."

"Simon works here," Rob told her now that his neurons were firing again. "He works in the bridal department. That's how he's targeting them. It's not the expo."

A pause, then Jo said, "So, it's just a coincidence that Yvette works there too?"

Rob sat down on a glass display containing wedding shoes. "I guess so. He got lucky."

He tried to think. Where would the stalker take Yvette? It would have to be somewhere deserted, somewhere they wouldn't be interrupted. It was still daylight, so he'd wait until dark before he...

He couldn't bear to think about that. He forced his thoughts back on track. If the stalker was waiting until dark, where would he hole up? In his car? Did he have a car? He must have done to get Yvette away from here.

He spoke into the phone. "Jo, see if you can find a car registered to Simon Burridge. He must have had one nearby in order to take her away. He couldn't have dragged her onto a bus or a tube."

"On it," barked Jo and he heard her issuing orders to someone in the room.

"It is possible he tricked her into going somewhere with him," he thought out loud. "But it's not his usual M.O."

"No, usually he takes them by surprise." A pause as she thought for a moment. "Rob, does Simon have a disability?"

"He's completely bald," Rob said. "Not shaved, but smooth, like no growth at all. That's not a big thing in itself, but it might have been when he was growing up. He probably got bullied because of it. He could have developed a complex."

"That would explain why he didn't have any girlfriends," said Jo. "Oh, hang on..."

Rob waited. He wanted to do something, go somewhere, but he didn't know where to start.

"Simon's phone is off, so no luck there, but Yvette's pinged a cell phone tower twenty minutes ago on Parkside, near Wimbledon Common."

"Right, I'm on my way." There were lots of heavily wooded areas in Wimbledon Common, lots of places to hide.

"I'll meet you in the Windmill carpark with the dog squad." She hung up.

He raced downstairs back to his car leaving the police officers and security staff in his wake. Almost immediately, his phone rang again, but he put it on speaker. It was Mallory. "Hey, Simon

Burridge drives a dark grey Honda Civic with the licence plate LP67 YCB. I've put out an all-points bulletin, so we've got everyone keeping an eye out. It was last clocked by the ANPR camera on the A219 going over Putney Bridge."

"He's heading towards Wimbledon Common," yelled Rob over the sirens.

"Uniform are on their way, along with the canine unit," said Mallory. "Don't worry, mate. We'll find her."

Rob swallowed. A lot could happen in twenty-minutes.

"I just hope we're not too late."

20

The stalker glanced over to where Yvette slumped unconscious in the passenger seat. The Rohypnol he'd slipped into her coffee during their tea break had done its work, she was out cold. It was so easy with vain women. He'd simply told her he wanted her to meet a friend who was looking for a model for a freelance job – bridal wear, of course – and she'd jumped at the chance.

At least now he could stop pretending. He'd heard just about enough of her relationship crisis, her fiancé's demanding job, the fact he was never home. He got that she felt neglected, but so fucking what? She should try being bullied every day at school for being the weirdo with no hair. Have the opposite sex laugh in her face and whisper derogative comments behind her back. Then, how would she feel?

She'd had a pampered life, she was beautiful, appreciated, with a body most men would ache to hold. He found her repulsive. She used her sexuality to ensnare men, tap into their weakness. Her fiancé was a classic case in point. She didn't love him, she only loved how he made her feel. Wanted. Appreciated. All the feelings he had never experienced, not even from his good-for-nothing parents. He gave a dry laugh. When you looked at it that way, he'd been doomed from the start. Not that he regretted it, not anymore. It had made him the person he was today. The hunter everybody feared.

The Surrey Stalker.

He still got goose-bumps thinking about the name they'd given him. It had such a fearsome ring to it. He'd go down in history as one of the county's most infamous serial killers, along with Robert Napper and Levi Bellfield. And he was just getting started.

Yvette was a perfect target being self-centred and superficial as well as engaged. Just like Bridget, she was tying herself to the wrong man. Oh, he had no doubt the intrepid detective Rob Miller was in love with her, he'd seen it on his face in the cocktail bar the other night. Little did he know he was about to make a massive mistake, the biggest of his life. He, the stalker, was doing Miller a favour by taking Yvette off his hands – and making her pay.

He gave a hollow laugh, he could thank him later.

Traffic was heavy up Putney Hill, which slowed him down, but he wasn't panicked. He didn't think anyone could trace him. His phone was off, no one knew his real name, and the idiot detective didn't have a clue who he was, even though he'd stared right at him the other night. The gay façade had worked wonders, it always did when he had to get close to his targets. They never suspected he was putting it on.

He drove around Tibbet's Corner roundabout onto Wimbledon Parkside when it struck him.

Her phone.

He couldn't believe he'd been stupid enough to forget about her fucking phone. Grimacing, he veered off the road and onto the hard shoulder, nearly side-swiping a motorcyclist. He reached across his drugged-up passenger and fished in her handbag for her mobile.

Where the hell was it? He eventually found it in a side-pocket. He smashed it on the dashboard to open it up, took out the sim card. He then threw both the phone and the sim out of the window into the dense vegetation that flanked the right-hand side of the road. He had no doubt her cop fiancé would try to ping it as soon as he discovered she was missing, but since she wasn't living with him at the moment – she'd told him in painstaking detail how she'd moved out – it was unlikely that had happened yet.

It was twilight when he turned into Windmill Road, which led to the centre of Wimbledon Common. It was dangerous parking there, but he needed to get his victim into the deep, dark woods. Robert Frost's poem had never been more apt.

The woods are lovely, dark and deep, But I have promises to keep, And miles to go before I sleep, And miles to go before I sleep.

He chanted the words to himself as he undid Yvette's seatbelt and tried to wake her up, enough so that she could walk. Carrying her would attract too much attention. When she didn't respond he slapped her through the face. She groaned and her eyes flickered open, but only momentarily before they shut again. Hell, he hadn't even given her that much, just enough to make her dozy, yet the stupid bitch had gone and passed out. He wacked her again.

"Wha–?" This time she turned her unfocused eyes onto him and he smiled as he saw the fear register in them.

"Time to go." He got out of the car, opened her door and helped her out. She leaned heavily on him, swaying dangerously, but somehow, he managed to close the door and support her as they walked in the direction of the trees. She was trying to talk but couldn't get the words out. To anyone watching, it would appear like he was taking his inebriated girlfriend for a much-needed stroll to clear her head.

She was heavier than he anticipated, and by the time they reached the trees he'd worked up quite a sweat.

That's okay, he thought. *It will be worth it when I get her under-cover. That's when she'll get what's coming to her.*

It was all he could do not to laugh with glee.

21

Rob raced down the narrow Windmill Road and hit the brakes once he got to the carpark at the bottom. Despite the late hour, there were still scraggly school children running about followed by harassed parents and overexcited dogs. He cruised up and down the aisles looking for the Honda Civic.

There!

It was parked at the edge of the carpark in the last bay in the last aisle. There were no other cars around it. Clearly, Simon hadn't wanted anyone to see him with Yvette.

They couldn't have gone far. Knowing Yvette, she would have been struggling or screaming, probably both. Then he frowned. No, he would have subdued her somehow since he couldn't afford for her to make a noise and attract attention. Maybe she was gagged? An image of Yvette lying on the ground, duct-tape over her mouth came to mind, but he pushed it firmly away. Not yet. He wouldn't go there just yet. There was still time.

He felt the Honda's bonnet, it was hot, and he smelled fuel and heard the faint ticking as the engine cooled down. Five, ten minutes at the most.

Rob took stock of the area. Behind him was the lodge which housed a popular lunchtime canteen, but since it was almost dark, the restaurant had shut and there were now only a scattering of people sitting at the wooden tables outside, cleaning off their boots or changing shoes before they went home. None of them would have seen anything since there were four rows of parked cars and about two hundred metres between where he stood and the restaurant.

In front of him was a large field crisscrossed with walking paths leading into the dark bank of trees around the exterior. Rob glanced up at the sky. He reckoned he had about twenty minutes of light left, then night would descend and with it, acts of horror that didn't bear thinking about. There were no lights in the carpark or the lane leading to it, and beneath the canopy of trees, it was already dark.

He set off on the path that led directly to the clump of trees up ahead. He'd been here once or twice before and knew the basic layout of the common. To his left, a steep path wound down to a crescent-shaped lake, but it was popular with walkers and the stalker would have to have passed an entire row of cars to get to it, so he didn't think he'd gone that way. He'd have been looking for the quickest and easiest route to the coverage of the trees, which meant straight ahead.

The temperature dropped once he got amongst the trees, and the sounds of the night replaced the children's laughter and dogs barking. Scurrying animals, chirping insects and creaking branches echoed off the sturdy oaks and plane trees around him.

"Yvette!" he yelled, hoping that she was still able to shout out, to scream, or give him an indication of where she was. His only reply was a squawking squirrel that dashed across the path in front of him, or at least he thought it was a squirrel. It was almost too dark to see.

He followed the path down, his senses hyper-alert, listening for any unnatural sounds – a man's boot, a thud or a gasp, but there was nothing. The path wound down to the left and became slippery and uneven. He moved to the side where he could get some traction on the tufts of grass along the edge.

"Yvette!"

Still nothing. Where the hell had Simon taken her? He must be around here somewhere. This was the most secluded part of the common. Anywhere else and he'd risk being seen. Rob decided to leave the path, but should he go left or right? He peered into the darkness, trying to put himself into the mind of the killer. The left was more uneven as it sloped down towards the lake. It would be slippery and damp. He chose the high ground on the right and stepped over broken branches and collapsed tree trunks as he made his way through the thick undergrowth.

"Yvette!" He tried again. This time he thought he heard something, a rustling that suddenly stopped. He inched his way closer, keeping his hands out in front of him to deter low branches rendered invisible by the darkness. "Are you here?"

There was a muffled response. A moan. Then he heard a slapping sound of skin on skin.

Bastard.

"Yvette, I'm coming!" He charged through the bush like a madman, following the direction of the moans and his instinct. Eventually, the foliage cleared, and he saw Yvette lying on the cold, hard ground, her wrists bound above her head and tied to a tree stump.

Above her was Simon.

Emitting a guttural yell, Rob charged the stalker, who was ready for him. The flying branch hit Rob across the forehead and knocked him off his feet. Growling, he scrambled to his knees and continued his forward trajectory in the direction of the stalker. "Get away from her."

There was another thwack as the branch came down again, and Rob lost consciousness.

ROB AWOKE to swirling leaves above him and an overwhelming sense of nausea. He blinked while his eyes adjusted and turned his head. The pain across his forehead and down his neck was excruciating, but through the red mist, he could see the supine figure of Yvette, a few metres away. He tried to roll over and found he couldn't move his arms. As his muddled brain struggled to kick-start, he realised he was bound to a tree, his arms above his head.

The stalker had now completely subdued Yvette, who wasn't moving. Rob stared at her chest to see if she was breathing and thought he detected the faint rise and fall of her breasts. Then, he realised with a start that her skirt was bunched up around her waist and the rapist was in the process of removing her underwear.

Rob growled and wrestled against the tape binding him. The stalker turned his head.

"Just in time."

Rob twisted his arms around and felt the tape give a little. A bit more twisting and wrenching and he thought he could get free. He pulled himself back along the ground towards the tree to which he was bound, until his face was under his hands. Then using his eyeteeth, he ripped the tape apart. After that, all it took was a firm twist and he was free.

The stalker obviously hadn't counted on an enraged man when he'd tied Rob up, he was used to women who he could overpower easily. With a furious yell, Rob threw himself at the stalker who fell sideways off Yvette. She barely moved. Rob punched him in the face and heard the satisfying crack as his nose or cheekbone broke, he wasn't sure which, and he didn't much care. The stalker roared and rolled to the side so Rob's second punch hit the dirt. Then he was up on his feet and charging. The two men went flying into the undergrowth. Rob barely felt the twigs and thistles beneath him as he rolled away from his attacker and scrambled to his feet. But the stalker kept coming, and this time landed a punch that made Rob see stars. The stalker was taller than he was, but not as broad, and Rob knew he could take him out in a fair fight. But there was nothing fair about this one. The stalker hit him again, sensing his advantage and Rob staggered, but managed to stay on his feet. With a growl, his attacker picked up a rock and brought it down on Rob's head. Luckily, Rob saw it coming and twisted to the side, so the force of the rock landed on his shoulder. The pain radiated down his back, releasing a surge of adrenalin. Rob moved forward, throwing punch after punch, oblivious to the pain or to anything else other than the man in front of him. The stalker fell to his knees, his nose spurting blood.

"How do you like that?" rasped Rob, punching him again.

The stalker fell back onto the ground. He still held the rock in his hand which he raised feebly in an attempt at self-defence. Rob grabbed the rock from his limp fingers and brought it down on his head. It smashed into his forehead with a sickening thud.

Somewhere behind him, Rob heard dogs barking and someone shouting. He hit the stalker again with the rock, then again, and again, until there was nothing left of his face but a bloody mess.

"Rob, that's enough." Jo's voice penetrated the thick mist that had encased him. "Drop the rock."

Rob did as she said and sat back on his haunches, panting. He felt her arms envelop him, and he dropped his head onto her shoulder. "It's okay," she breathed. "You got him. Yvette is safe now."

Yvette!

Rob turned to see a huddle of paramedics leaning over her body. "Is she...?"

"She's alive," Jo said, still holding him in her arms. "He didn't rape her."

"Thank God."

Rob let himself melt against her, the fight draining out of him. Suddenly, he felt cold, really cold, and began to shiver.

"It's okay," Jo said, not moving. "I've got you."

She turned to someone hovering behind her. "Can I have a blanket?"

A fleecy blanked was draped around them. How long they stayed that way, Rob didn't know, but when the mist and the pain cleared long enough to see properly, he stared disbelievingly at the bloodied head of Simon Burridge as a team of pathologists lit up the area all around them.

"Did I do that?"

"Yeah." Jo hesitated. "Do you think you can stand up?"

He nodded, feeling the pain radiate down his neck and into his shoulder. "I think I've bust my collarbone."

"We'll get you looked at just as soon as we can. You've got a nasty bump on your forehead too."

"The bastard hit me with a branch."

"Okay, come on." She got to her feet, her arm still firmly around his back. He leaned on her until he was sure his legs could take his weight. "I've got you."

Together, they walked unsteadily up the path to the carpark where an ambulance was waiting. Actually, there were three ambulances, but only one was for him.

"Let's sit you down," a paramedic said kindly. With Jo's help, Rob fell rather than sat onto the ledge at the back of the ambulance. Immediately, the paramedic inspected his head wound. "That's a big bump."

Rob nodded, then wished he hadn't. He closed his eyes against the pain. "Thanks for finding us," he said to Jo, who was standing in front of him looking rather pale herself.

"It was the sniffer dogs. I wouldn't have had a clue where you were. How on earth did you find them?"

"I found his car and took the most direct route into the woods, then I left the path for the dense area on the high ground and shouted for Yvette. I think I got lucky, because she moaned, before she passed out."

"Bloody lucky," she hissed beneath her breath. "Any later and..."

He hung his head. "I know."

"Look into the light." The medic shone a torch into his eyes. Rob blinked and tried to focus, but all he could concentrate on was the pain in his shoulder.

"You've got a concussion," said the medic seriously. "And your collar bone is broken. I'll have to take you to the hospital for treatment."

"What about the stalker?" Rob glanced at Jo's face.

She sighed. "Well, you did quite a number on him. He's not going anywhere except the morgue. I won't say he didn't deserve it, but there will be an enquiry."

Rob nodded. Unavoidable, really, given the circumstances. He had beaten the guy to death with a rock.

"But, given your own injuries, and the seriousness of the situation, I think you'll probably get off with a minor suspension. I doubt it'll mean the end of your career. I mean, you caught the Surrey Stalker, for God's sake. That's got to count for something."

Rob grimaced. "Yes, I did." *Before I killed him.*

"And we'll be able to match his fingerprints to the partials we got from the duct-tape, not that it matters now, but that will prove he was responsible for Julie and Sara's murders."

"It matters," he muttered. Both women deserved justice, they all did.

"I'm sorry I lost it," he said. "If I'd controlled myself, he might have confessed to Bridget's murder, and the Yorkshire girl, Greta. Now there isn't a way to link him to their deaths." He thought about poor Ron Studley behind bars and sighed. He'd let him down.

"Not necessarily," said Jo. "I've sent a team over to Simon's apartment. You never know, he might have kept a memento of Bridget, something we can use to connect him to the case? She was the love of his life, after all."

It was a possibility. "I hope so," he said. "For that poor bugger's sake."

"Let's get that arm stable." The medic moved in solicitously. Rob let him put his arm in a sling and accepted some painkillers. Jo hovered nearby, keeping a watchful eye.

"Thanks, Jo, for everything." He reached out and squeezed her hand. She didn't resist. "Anytime."

He grimaced, releasing her. "Let's hope there's not a next time."

A team of paramedics appeared out of the woods carrying a stretcher. Yvette lay in it, groggy, but alive.

"She's going to be fine," said Jo, then she dropped her voice. "You could have told me you were engaged. I never would have..."

"I know," he interjected, meeting her gaze. "That's why I didn't tell you."

She nodded and sat down beside him in the ambulance.

They watched as Yvette was wheeled into a separate ambulance and secured in place. Then the doors closed, and the vehicle took off, sirens blaring.

DCI Lawrence strode up to them.

"Well done, Rob. I've just seen what you did to our perp at the crime scene."

His crime scene.

"I'm sorry, I..."

"It's okay, I know it was self-defence. I heard you took quite a beating. Are you okay?"

Rob grinned, relieved. "I'll live."

"Glad to hear it. Are you going to the hospital? I can give you a lift if you like, I'm sure she'd like to see you." They all knew who he meant.

"Yeah," he got to his feet, still a little wobbly.

"You sure you're okay?" Lawrence frowned, supporting him under the arm. "You are entitled to your own ambulance, you know?"

He chuckled. "No need, I'm fine. You heard the medic, it's just a little concussion and a popped collar bone, nothing major."

The medic snorted. "Make sure you get yourself checked out at the hospital."

Lawrence nodded. "Okay, tough guy. Let's go."

Jo stood up. "Well, I'll say goodbye. I've got to go back to the station and pack up. Case closed."

"Excellent teamwork, Jo." Lawrence shook her hand. "And a great result. We bloody got him. I can't wait to let the press know."

"Thank you, sir."

He moved away, giving them some space. "Whenever you're ready, Rob."

Rob turned to Jo. "I'm sorry." He nodded toward the departing figure of his boss. "I have to go to the hospital, Yvette needs me."

She waved him away. "Don't be. I'm cool with it. You go and be with your fiancé, and I'll see you around."

Still neither of them moved.

"Can I at least give you a hug?" Rob didn't want to leave her, but he knew he had to. He had to choose, and Yvette was his fiancé, and she needed him more now than she ever had before. He couldn't desert her.

Through sickness and in health.

Jo broke into a grin. "I thought you'd never ask."

He wrapped his arms around her and held her close. "I don't regret it," he said softly into her hair.

She clung to him for a moment, as if she also didn't want to let go, but then she released him. "Go on now, and don't forget to get your head and shoulder looked at."

"Yes, ma'am," he said, and hobbled after Lawrence who was waiting in the car. When he turned back to wave, she was already gone.

If you enjoyed *The Surrey Stalker* and you'd like to read more from this author, follow B.L. Pearce on Amazon.

THE REVENGE KILLER

DCI ROB MILLER #2

A brutal stabbing puts DCI Rob Miller on the trail of a serial revenge killer in this gritty, suspenseful thriller from Amazon bestselling author B.L. Pearce.

The body of a man is found in a residential home in west London. He's been stabbed to death in what appears to be a frenzied rage attack. Newly promoted and recently married DCI Rob Miller is assigned the case.

As Rob delves into the victim's past, he discovers the known felon was under surveillance by the National Crime Agency, who send their latest recruit, Rob's ex-lover, Jo Maguire, to work with him on the case. When a second man is murdered with the same M.O. it becomes obvious the two deaths are linked.

The investigation leads them to London's undercover sex industry and as they get more involved, they quickly realise that the murderer is leaving a blistering trail of revenge killings that are only going to escalate. Can DCI Miller and Jo work together to stop the murderer before he kills again?

Available from Amazon

ABOUT THE AUTHOR

BL Pearce is a British crime writer and author of the DCI Rob Miller series.

B.L. Pearce grew up in post-apartheid Southern Africa. As a child, she lived on the wild eastern coast and explored the sub-tropical forests and surfed in shark-infested waters. She attended university in Cape Town during the protests and on more than one occasion rode through burning tyres and riots in order to get to lectures. She was also present at Nelson Mandela's inauguration.

She moved to London with her family after gaining a post-graduate degree in Business Science, but South Africa has left an indelible mark. The poverty and desperation, the crime and corruption, as well as the exquisite natural beauty and awe-inspiring wildlife, will always be a part of her, and will probably always feature in her novels in one way or another.